EVE

IMMORTAL STORIES VOLUME 1

GENE DOUCETTE

FOREWORD

Immortal Stories: Eve is about a character from the *Immortal novel series: Immortal, Hellenic Immortal and Immortal at the Edge of the World*. This story takes place following the events in *Immortal at the Edge of the World*.

Reading the novels prior to reading *Eve* is recommended, but not mandatory—the story stands on its own.

Please refer to the conclusion of this book for more information on the *Immortal* novels and on the ongoing novella series *The Immortal Chronicles*.

ONE

"Your name?"

The man asking the question had three visible piercings—ears and nose—and a tattoo that ran down his right arm, with a hint that it continued beneath the shirt and up to the shoulder. He wore a close-cropped beard and had long hair tied back by a rubber band.

He was an echo of a half-dozen warrior cultures, and this made him difficult to look at directly.

"My name?" she asked.

"Yeah, for the order."

He held a paper cup aloft to help her understand, as if she perhaps didn't speak the language. A black marker was in his other hand.

I mean to inscribe your name on the cup, he was saying.

It wasn't that she didn't comprehend the question, it was that she didn't know how to respond. Handing over her name—any name—was an unexpected complication, because she had not yet decided what she was going to be calling herself. The purchase of a beverage was supposed to be an anonymous transaction, one that didn't require her to make such an important so soon.

What was the name they gave me? she thought. Perhaps that would do for the moment.

"Eve," she said. "Write that. I'm sure I will remember it."

He frowned, scribbled the name, and then passed the cup down to a busy-looking woman. He then recited a number, which Eve took to be a declaration of cost.

She pulled a bill from her pocket and handed it over, in exchange for which she received several other bills and some coins.

It wasn't really as mysterious to her as all that. She understood the number system involved, and the notion of currency as recompense for goods and services was an idea almost as old as society. It was only that the numbers had no objective reality behind them. The specialty drink she had requested could have been associated with any number; she had no real-world connection to it as a value to compare to another thing. That same amount could have also been the cost of a house or a bicycle or a piece of gum.

It wasn't that she had no perspective on the expense of a cup of coffee either; it was that she had too much. She knew the cost of an equivalent cup when the drink was exotic and rare, and also when it was a mundane afterthought.

In this instance, the value associated with what she had purchased appeared to have less to do with scarcity or novelty, and more with assumptions made regarding the uniqueness of its preparation. This, too, was almost as old as society.

Our fire is the better fire, she thought. *Our wood burns warmer.*

The man behind the counter caught her smile, and responded positively. Eve had the kind of smile that could do that to other people.

"You look like you just thought of a good joke," he said. This was not a part of his rehearsed patter. It had no commercial intent.

"I was thinking of a very old political campaign."

"Oh." He looked a little bewildered, then snapped back into his role as a corporate extension. "Your drink will come up over there. They'll call you."

"Yes of course, thank you."

She stepped aside so the next in an overlong line could proceed.

There was an approximately equal balance between the service region of the shop and the clientele space—a seemingly haphazard collection of tables and chairs, with a temporally discordant fireplace/leather chairs arrangement against one wall.

It was moments like this that reminded her why she found the modern world so dizzying so often, and why it was easier to simply step away for decades at a time. Being fully present in this reality meant resigning herself to a perpetual dull ache. Here was a modern twenty-first century coffee shop with a decorative piece that belonged in a hunting lodge or a wayside tavern from centuries past, when men were always armed and that armament was always a sharp piece of metal. The fireplace was there, she supposed, to connect the patrons with a sense of welcome, a *home and hearth* ethic, but it was so artificial, and ignorant of the unlikelihood that any patron legitimately associated their child-hood with a fireplace, it had no meaning.

It also had no function. The building had its own internal heat source, no doubt, and even if it hadn't, it was summer and the sun was unrelenting, warming the room through the windows.

Of small consolation, all the occupants—the room was half-full—were still armed with sharp bits of metal. It was only that those bits of metal were electronic devices and not knives or swords. Weapons of a less literal sort.

Eve took a seat at a table near one of the windows. The shop was adjacent to a busy street, on the other side of which was a grassy bank beside a narrow river. She could see oarsmen on the water, skipping a scull along the surface and mimicking volun-tarily an act that would have only been performed by a slave for most of human history. But then that seemed to her like the definition of most sporting events: a deliberate, competitive parody of feats historically accomplished unwillingly by the lower class or the owned.

Next to the river, some people walked gently, together or alone, while others ran.

Jogged, she corrected herself. *Not fleeing or hunting. Running to run.*

This, at least, she could support. Humans were meant to run.

Then there was the road, which was a relentless blur of cars and trucks racing by with a kind of fury that reminded her of a stampede.

We slew the mammoths, and then we became the mammoths.

She shut her eyes and tried to refocus. It was too much, too fast. The world was an overwhelming onslaught of stimuli. She was getting dizzy.

I should have started smaller.

"Eve?"

She turned at the sound of the name. It would always ring unfamiliar, she decided. But it had been centuries since she had used *any* proper name, so the possibility was real she would never find one that adequately summed up who she thought of herself as.

Her coffee drink was ready. She retrieved it, and returned to the table.

The drink was a thing whose name she dimly recognized as Italian: Latte. It was actually Turkish, but she liked to imagine the Romans having their hands on this sort of drink. Knowing the Romans, they'd have erected statues and developed a minor religion to honor it. Or perhaps they would keep it secret and for use only in ceremony or for their Emperors, like chocolate in the Americas.

It was bitter, and too hot, but she appreciated it from the perspective of a mandatory ritual. It was what one did when joining—or rejoining—society: find out where the people congregate, and go there. Partake in their customs. Acclimatize.

~

A cloud passed over the sun and darkened the firmament long enough for the lights inside the shop to out-perform the outside light, and then Eve was eye-to-eye with her reflection for the first time in ages.

She had a striking face. Her skin was desperately pale, her eyes a bright blue, her hair a tangled, vibrant mess of red. She had high cheekbones and a narrow, flat nose that—in times when noses were an important feature—stood out as unfortunately petite.

In most cultures, in most histories, she was beautiful. In a dozen or so, she was the literal paragon of beauty. In five or six, she was an actual goddess.

But it was also just her face. It was the one she always saw staring back in mirrors, in pools of water, in the eyes of lovers. Sometimes it looked a little different, but it was always the same face to her. Which was to say that although it had been decades since she'd seen her own reflection, there were no surprises.

This is not where to look for something new, she thought, turning away from the window and toward the crowded shop.

A Chinese girl sat at a nearby table. She had a round face and bright eyes and a shy smile. Her shoulders were hunched as she leaned over her coffee and spoke to a companion—a white male with blond hair and the kind of facial scruff children have before they can grow full beards.

The girl's posture was alarming.

Eve imagined a wood switch slapping the girl across the knuckles as an angry teacher with perfect posture and perfect make-up chastised her. *Straighten your back. The geisha is elegance and strength and smallness. Where is your honor?*

"Where is your honor?" Eve repeated quietly.

The girl ignored the phantom's chastisement, and didn't hear Eve's.

As the Chinese girl spoke to the European conqueror at her opposite, her hand described precise characters in a notebook. Numbers, perhaps, or letters, or that odd combination of the two that constituted advanced mathematics. Knowledge, in either case.

The boy sat back in his chair and waited for her to finish speaking, and then responded with a question, prompting her to speak some more. Eve realized the Chinese girl was the teacher and her European friend was the pupil.

How remarkable.

At another table, a distressingly rotund man sat alone before a computer device and typed in sporadic rapid bursts. He wore black pants and boots and a large blue t-shirt. A vague sweat odor came off of him that was detectable from half a room away, possibly because the day was warm but his apparel didn't reflect that reality. He had some sort of dirt or grease in the creases of his joints—his neck, his elbows—and under his fingernails.

She could see him manning a carriage with a slew of equipment—buckets, shovels and lamps, an overcoat, a mask—and riding about polluted London in the dark, his lantern bouncing in time with the nag that pulled his shop.

He's a night soil man, surely.

But no, the smell was not quite so bad as that, the filth on his person not all that filthy, and the profession itself no longer of use. There was still an interest in this world for the geisha, but the night soil man's time had passed.

He was still an oddity. The computer was supposed to be an indicator of some affluence, but—and this was always so, even when mankind was no larger than the sum of the persons in this shop—the affluent were always cleaner, and healthier. If the man with the laptop wasn't a professional filth aggregator, his appearance indicated that he was a beggar.

He looked unhealthy.

The last observation could have been extended to nearly everyone there, though. With only a few exceptions, this odd collection of humanity was full of the sick and the damaged. In the corner near the inactive fireplace a woman with a mole on her face and two missing teeth was complaining to the man she was with about her job. Eve could pick up no more than a word or two, but understood already that this was as close as the woman would ever get to happiness. She had been damaged, possibly at a very early age, and that damage—whatever it was— would hold her short of fulfillment for her entire life.

A man near the door stood only with the help of a brace and a crutch. He had a crippling disorder of some sort. Looking at him triggered no historical counterpart for Eve, because there were almost none to draw from. When children were born like this, they didn't live to adulthood except if they were by chance also royalty. Most of the deformed were dealt with upon delivery, with a rock. And adult males who couldn't hunt or run served no use except as bait, or only very occasionally as a font of wisdom.

This was how the world used to work. Eve didn't make it that way, but she knew how it was.

She closed her eyes again.

This isn't why you're here, she reminded herself.

These were observations she'd been making of the human condition for century upon century, most times at a safe remove. It was possible to extract herself from the daily reality the rest of the world was forced to slog through, to watch from afar. She wasn't there to watch, though, she was there to experience.

But being in the middle of it was so much worse than she remembered. It was noisier and smellier than it should have been. Everything was too heavy and the clothing itched. She wanted to leave.

This is your world, not mine, she thought. *I have no part here.*

She sipped her coffee, and didn't go.

~

*H*er opinion on the quality of the coffee changed for the positive as it began to cool. Also, someone was staring at her. This had no impact on how she felt about the coffee but it improved—marginally—her opinion regarding the people sharing the room.

He was a tall, ebony man with no hair on his head, dressed simply in a sleeveless shirt and a pair of shorts, with the bright rubbery shoes of an athlete. Normal convention would indicate he was either preparing to perform a physical feat of some sort or had just returned from one. She assumed he would be sweaty if the latter was the case. Then she imagined what he might look like glistening with sweat.

He wasn't the only person in the shop to steal glances at her. The large man with the laptop looked her way every tenth heartbeat, and there was a woman next to the emergency exit who not only kept looking at Eve but had twice taken her picture with the camera on her cellular phone. Mostly, Eve ignored this kind of attention. People had been telling her exactly how beautiful she was since the invention of language. It may have been immodest to recognize this to such a degree, to take it so entirely for granted, but she was also older than modesty. Recognizing that she should wear clothing in public places was the extent of her interest in social norms in this regard.

She knew, in other words, that she drew eyes, and had no particular concern with it. What was different about the dark-skinned warrior staring at her from the coffee bar was that she was happy to have caught his gaze. She was staring back, and for much the same reason.

It's been a long time, she thought. *I nearly forgot what this felt like.*

His eyes met hers, and quickly turned away—*I've been caught staring*—then back again upon the discovery that she'd not averted her gaze. He gave the slightest of smiles.

When his drink was ready, he pointed to the chair opposite her, his eyebrows forming the unspoken question.

She nodded, and waved him over.

"Hi," he said, sliding into the seat. He had a deep baritone. It was the voice men heard when they wrote poems about thunder gods. "I'm sorry, you caught me staring but I feel like... do we know each other?"

"No," she said. "I didn't *catch* you staring, you were only staring and I saw you and stared back."

"So you did, so you did." He smiled broadly, but his eyes still looked terribly confused. "But we've never met?"

"Do you suppose, had we met before, you'd have forgotten?"

He looked down at the table, and up again. He rubbed his face. He appeared deeply perplexed.

"No, I definitely would have remembered you. So... I'm Rick. You are... Eve?" He had tilted his head to read her coffee cup. "Eve or 'eye'."

"Eve is what you can call me."

"Good, calling you 'Eye' would've been a little weird, huh?"

"Yes, it would have."

He rubbed his face some more.

"So, um, this still seems really... weird."

"You keep using that word."

"Yeah, I know. Are... you from around here?"

"I am not. I'm visiting."

He seemed so uncomfortable. She understood that there was a modicum of introductory small talk that needed to be performed in this situation. Every tribe had customs. But it seemed obvious why she'd waved him over and what she was interested in. Now he was here and the confidence she found appealing was gone. Rick had strong, broad shoulders and rippling chest muscles she could trace even with them hidden under his shirt, but he was slouching like the Chinese girl now. It was beyond understanding.

"Oh, yes? From where?"

"Are *you* from around here?" she asked. "You look as if you're about to go do something athletic."

"Oh I am, but no, no I wasn't. I was gonna take a walk maybe, but I dress like this. A lot. In the summer, you know. It's warm out."

"Yes I know." She was wearing a skirt and sandals, with a simple peasant blouse and an undershirt. It was clothing she found assembled on a store mannequin, and took the combination to be a contemporary representation of appropriate attire.

Clothing was one of the reasons she hated stepping out of the veil. It wasn't so much that society largely frowned upon nudity —although this too was a convention she barely understood—it was the degree of complication implicit in clothing choice. She didn't dislike clothes. She wore them quite often. But the difference between period-appropriate clothing and outrageously incorrect clothing could be as tiny as a scarf or a brooch. In certain eras, to fit in she had to learn how to master five or six layers for the honor of sweltering in the midday sun. It often simply wasn't worth it.

She was thankful that those days had mostly passed, and modern people dressed in ways that were slightly more rational. It meant she could wear nothing but a skirt and a thin top, and Rick could dress in less clothing than a Greek on his way to the baths, and neither would be accosted.

"But yeah," he said. "I live around the corner. Where'd you say you were from?"

"I didn't say."

"You have a really interesting accent, it's hard to place."

"It would be, for your ears. Where I'm from no longer exists."

He nodded slowly. "So, ah, war refugee?"

She smiled. "That's a good way of putting it, yes."

"Eastern Europe, maybe?"

She was much, much older than Europe. For the first third of her life Europe was uninhabited, and partly uninhabitable because of glaciers. She decided not to share this.

"Africa, actually."

His eyebrows went up. "Africa?"

"Originally, yes."

"South Africa?"

"Continentally, somewhere in the middle. But it was a long time ago."

"So…look I don't want to offend you, but you're maybe the whitest person I've ever seen."

"I suppose I am."

She had been living on the other side of the veil for a long time, and that contributed to the pallor of her skin, but she didn't tell him that. Her skin and hair color could change at her whim, given time. It tended to default to the shade of the creatures around her.

"That just doesn't scream Africa to me," he said. "Sorry, again, I don't want to offend you."

"What you say is not offensive. As I said, this was a long time ago."

Race was something that had been invented when she wasn't paying attention. It was created to justify violence, and like so many other justifications, Eve had trouble believing it still existed. But again, this wasn't the world she wanted, it was the world she was left with.

The idea that someone who looked as she looked could come from mid-continental Africa was clearly jarring, and as much as she wished to address that point—it was more accurate to say that the people from Africa came from *her*, for instance, than to say that she came from there—she recognized the subject as something on which it was unsafe to dwell.

"Right," he said. "So what happened to them?"

"Who?"

"Your… people, I guess. Your village or city, or…"

"My people were all killed. All the men, that is to say. We lost a war."

"That's awful! Did I read about it?"

"No, as I said—"

"—it was a long time ago, yeah. So, I'm from around here."

"You've said so."

"Yeah I mean, I'm American. No war stories for me."

"There have been a lot of American wars."

"Oh sure, just none involving me."

She considered asking if his ancestors had arrived in the country as slaves, but decided this too was an unsavory subject.

It was difficult to keep track of the idea that the things which happened only recently in her mind happened generations ago for everyone else. From her perspective, the present time they all shared was experiencing, at best, a temporary cease-fire. There had been thousands of such eras in history, and at the end of them empires always fell and the savage nature of mankind always resurfaced, took what it could and destroyed everything else.

She wanted to be wrong. She had yet to be.

"Do you work?" she asked. It was becoming quickly apparent that normal conversation was going to be at least as complicated as understanding the fashion of the period. Perhaps more. She couldn't steal appropriate conversational points from a store mannequin.

"I do! I'm a broker. Not on Sundays, though!" He gave a little laugh. She wondered if this was a Sunday. Days of the week were another thing she had to acquaint herself with. They were recent concepts. She understood them well enough, but the work-week notion, and specifically the idea of the weekend, was completely strange. She recalled Sundays being of some importance to certain religions, and wondered if she should go to a church to see what kind of people she'd meet there.

It wasn't likely to be as interesting as the coffee shop. A larger congregation, perhaps, but with greater homogeneity.

"You're a broker of… deals?" she asked.

"You could say so, sure. Stock broker."

She shrugged. These words didn't mean anything together.

"What do you do?" he asked.

"I don't do anything."

"Dead-end job, huh?'

"No, I don't have a job. I was thinking of getting one, though. I've been traveling for a long while and had no need of a profession until now."

"I guess you *have* been. And you're settling down here?"

"It's where I decided to stop moving. I haven't decided yet whether to stay, I may not like it. I only just arrived. Everything is very loud to me right now."

He nodded, but without understanding.

"But you have money," he said. "I mean you must, if you were traveling all that time. Takes a lot of money to travel."

"No it doesn't. You just start walking. Like those people over there, near the river."

"What do you do when you stop, people just feed you?"

It had been so long.

"No, I just… yes, I guess that's true. People just feed me." It *wasn't* true, but a lie was easier.

He nodded again. "Okay. Okay, that's cool. Did they just feed you here?"

"No, I gave them money."

"So you *do* have money."

"I went and found some before I arrived. But it will run out and then I'll have to find a job, as I said."

"Or just… *find* some more money?"

"I'm trying to do this without… traveling. I'd have to travel to find more money."

"Honest to God, this is the strangest conversation I've ever had."

"I'm sorry, it's difficult to explain. If I elaborated it would only create additional questions whose answers you would find even less satisfying."

"No, it's okay. It's interesting, at least."

"I'm very sorry, Rick, this is more talking than I expected us to have," she said. "I hadn't prepared."

He smiled. "Okay, we don't have to talk. I can just finish my coffee and get outta here."

"Oh, but… I thought that much at least was obvious. Perhaps I'm more out of touch than I realized."

"What, now?"

"Perhaps you are spoken for? That must be where my confusion is. I should have asked before now, I realize."

"Am I…"

"Are you beholden? Monogamy is disorienting, but I can respect it. Cultural norms are what they are. If there's a woman or a man you're exclusive with…?"

"All right, the conversation just got stranger."

"Is there?"

He coughed. "No, no there isn't, it's just… are you for real right now?"

"I'm real, yes."

"I'm not spoken for or… no, I'm single, Eve, but I'm not real clear on what you're saying here."

"I did think that part was obvious. I find you attractive. I don't believe I'm mistaken in your attraction to me."

"Um… no, you're not wrong."

"You have a place with privacy? I understand public intercourse is poorly taken."

"This is a joke, right? There's a camera somewhere or something? Am I being punked?"

Eve didn't know what *being punked* was and had no idea why this was all so difficult. She'd only decided to stay tethered to this dirty, smelly part of the world a few hours earlier, and already she was experiencing all the old aches and needs she remembered —fondly and less so—from when she lived in this world all the time. There was hunger, and thirst, and the baser bodily functions that came with food and drink. Soon there would be a need for sleep. And when she saw Rick, she remembered lust.

"This is the simplest thing imaginable, Rick."

"No, it's really not. We hardly know one another."

She laughed. "I'm not asking for a life mate. I have a biological need, and you look nicely compatible. But if I'm mistaken, I apologize. I may have more to understand about... about being here than I thought."

He didn't say anything. He just stared at her as if expecting something to happen that would explain the matter to his satisfaction.

"I'm sorry to have bothered you," she said, getting to her feet.

He caught her by the wrist.

"Wait," he said. "Just a second. If you're completely serious... like I said I only live around the corner."

"I am completely serious. I don't know how else to say that."

"Well all right. Then let's go."

TWO

The coffee shop was at the edge of a small parking lot primarily meant for use by a food market and an electronics retailer. The main entry to the lot was from the roadway with the cars driving far too quickly, but there was a small entrance/exit in the back behind the market. Past that small tributary of a road was a neighborhood.

Eve was always fascinated by the variety of humanity's living space choices. She'd seen everything, from standalone portable huts, to permanent interlocked structures that were vertically independent of one another, to freestanding, uniquely designed buildings. Sometimes it looked as if the architects were having a quiet argument with one another via structural design and color palettes.

At least we got out of caves.

She recalled an entire city in an underground maze of caves and tunnels and caverns that, for all she knew, still existed. The memory made her shiver.

Rick walked as though he was still confused. He didn't appear to know whether to travel ahead of her or beside her, to touch her or keep his distance. She wanted to see the man that first strode into the shop with an arrogance of superiority, but what she was getting was a confused child, and it was only making the entire matter more frustrating.

There had been changes. Eve understood this well enough. The kind of warrior mentality she was aching to tap into was the same mentality that too often resulted in violence and rape, and that was *not* what she wanted to revive, in anyone. But she'd offered herself as clearly and obviously as she could while still adhering to the ground rules of public behavior, and he still acted as though she was going to run off or scream for help.

"It's right up here," he said, pointing to an indistinct tomato-colored house. "I've got the second floor. Used to be one of those big one-family places, but they converted it to condos a few years back. I think they're trying to make the attic into a one bedroom space, but I don't know if there's a... sorry, I'm rambling. You okay?"

"I'm fine."

"Good, okay. Watch your step."

There was a small recess in the sidewalk that could sprain the ankle of someone unwary. It wasn't the sort of thing to panic over. She stepped past it, as she imagined she would have without the forewarning.

She thought back to a time when she became enamored of a soldier participating in one of the Napoleonic wars. It was impossible to say what struck her about him. He was large, brutish and confident, but not handsomely chiseled, and not otherwise rakish or clever. She wanted him nonetheless, and so, after a particularly gruesome battle—which battle, what field it transpired upon, or how it ended she couldn't say—Eve appeared to him in a clearing near his tent.

From his perspective she was a magical woman who had arrived from another world, and he was afraid, right up until she asked him to bed her. He quickly overcame his fear, tossed her over his shoulder and carried her into his tent. They made love on the ground amidst muck and upturned soil.

It was a fond memory. She couldn't remember the name of the soldier, but she could still smell the mud from the field.

The Frenchman thought she was probably a devil, but had no issue engaging in sex with one when presented an opportunity. Rick, a citizen of a less superstitious age, undoubtedly did not think this of her. But was showing no imperative. Rather than warn her of cracks in the sidewalk, he could have picked her up in those long arms and taken her inside. The closest he had come, so far, was to offer to carry her bag.

His hands betrayed a small tremble when unlocking the door that led to the entryway, and he kept looking over his shoulder to make sure she was still there. She could step into the veil if she wanted and—from his perspective—effectively disappear. He was acting like he knew this to be a real possibility.

Once inside, they went up the open hallway stairs to another locked door and more fumbling, and then they were in his private space.

"It's not much," he said," and it's a mess, but I didn't think I'd be picking up a girl with my coffee."

It was a room with a couch and a television, a dining table and chairs, a small side area with cooking appliances, and two doors: presumably, a bedroom and a bathroom.

There were loose articles of clothing on the floor of the living room, plus a hamper of folded clothing and linens on the couch.

She forgot how much clothing people were accustomed to having in these times. All she had was a small duffel bag with three sets of clothing and a second pair of shoes. The remaining contents of the bag was paper money, which she decided she might have to use to obtain more clothing, or a place to live, or both. It depended on how much the money could get her.

Rick continued to act incredibly nervous, and began picking up his clothes while pointing out features of his small living area.

"This is the living room, and the bedroom's through there, bathroom's over there if you need it." He flung a handful of clothes in a pile near the bedroom door. "Are you hungry? Table's new, I never even ate at it, but…"

In the time it had taken him to pick up, she'd gotten out of her clothing.

"…oh," he said.

"I chose apparel that was easy to remove," she said. "There is no hurry, if yours requires more effort. Take your time."

"Do you want to…" he pointed to the bedroom, still mostly speechless. It wasn't entirely dissimilar to the way he was staring at her before, only this time he appeared to be a good deal more incapacitated, and he wasn't looking at her eyes so much any longer.

Eve had always been athletic, and thin, with breasts large enough to draw the eye but small enough so she could run without being in a great deal of pain. There had been many centuries in which her physique was less than the feminine ideal, but the world of her birth was one in which women were as much hunters and warriors as they were nurturers and mothers. This was the body she had, and would always have. But even when larger women were preferred, she long ago learned that men were far less choosy about the shape of the woman before them if that woman had already gone through the trouble of removing her clothing.

He still hadn't moved, and apparently gave up on the sentence he was in the middle of.

"For Baal's sake, Rick."

She stepped up beside him. He was much taller. If he wished, he could pick her up and bend her in half. She rather wanted him to do exactly that.

She rubbed her bare chest against his stomach, and her hand on the front of his shorts. "You're erect, I see. Do you need me to help you out of the clothes, or are you familiar with how this works?"

~

*I*t had been a long time. Eve didn't fully realize exactly *how* long until later, when she had a moment to think, do some math, and work out that the Frenchman in the Napoleonic Wars may well have been the last time she'd laid with a man. Because the clocks moved at a different pace on the other side of the veil, it hadn't been a full two centuries for her, but still: it had been a long while.

Fortunately, once he got over his shyness, Rick proved fully capable of the task.

They took a couple of short breaks. The first was to get out of the living room and into the bedroom, where the bed offered more rambunctious opportunities than the couch or any of the other surfaces. (She did try and guide him toward the kitchen counter, which looked like the perfect height for someone of his stature, but he resisted and they ended up on the floor instead.) The second was to get water, and so he could locate additional condoms.

To that point, he couldn't have gotten her pregnant or sick, as she wasn't capable of either condition, but she understood his unwillingness to proceed unprotected.

Rick was generous. It would have been fair to say they'd only performed *the act* only a small number of times by the metric of his climaxes, but she saw no reason to stop just because he had spent himself, so she didn't. And when he understood this he was happy to assist, with a finger, or a tongue, or a thigh, knee or toe. She enjoyed as much of him as she could until he was ready again to engage her more traditionally.

It was perhaps two hours before exhaustion presented them with a natural resting point.

"Mercy," he said. He was lying on his back and she on hers. His hand was between her legs, but he was so tired his fingers were only helping because she was holding them there. She had just trembled through an orgasm that made the one before it feel like little more than a precursor, a modest temblor before the major quake. When it hit she had to arch her back and lift her hips into the air, legs open and words in dead languages spilling from her lips.

"Yes," she whispered. "A break will be fine."

"I can't keep up with you."

She laughed. "You kept up better than most."

He propped himself upon an elbow and took a good look at her. His earlier fear and trepidation had been replaced largely by wonder.

"Oh my *goodness*," he said, "you laughed! I didn't think I'd hear that. And a smile too."

He kissed her on the cheek, then climbed out of the bed and exited the room.

He had a leonine quality to his movements when he got to his feet, and his firm behind and the coiled muscles of his back made for a wondrous visual spectacle. It made her hungry again.

She rolled off the bed.

Rick didn't have a proper window in his bedroom. What he had instead was a sliding glass door with a long curtain, on the other side of which was a small porch.

It was getting dark.

She slid open the door and let the light breeze cool her off and dry the sweat. It felt nice, so she stepped out onto the porch.

There wasn't much of a view. She could see a small square of grass that constituted the private yard belonging to the property, personalized with bits of plastic furniture. The yard was contained by a tall, chain-link fence, just in case anyone was concerned about exactly where the ownership diverged. Directly across and to the left and right were other houses. The people in the yard to the left were cooking meat on an open flame. The smell reminded her of a more literal hunger.

"I'm not sure if I'm gonna get complaints from the neighbors or compliments, if you're gonna stand out there like that."

"The clothing here is scratchy," she said, turning around but remaining where she was. "I prefer not to wear it." The man watching his meats cook would have a decent view of her back if he chose to gaze in the right direction.

Rick was sitting on the edge of the bed and looking at her. He had the courtesy to not put on any clothing, but was also not prepared to step out on the porch with her while unclothed.

"*Here.* You keep saying things like that. How did the clothes feel when you were doing all this traveling of yours? Wherever that was?"

"It was looser and softer. When I wore clothing."

"Right. So how many is *most*?"

"I don't understand your question."

"You said I keep up better than most."

"Oh that, yes."

"I… I'm sorry, I just realized how rude that was. Something about you made me think I could ask… no, forget it."

"It's all right. I am trying to think how to quantify my response, but… it would have to be several hundred. I never bothered to count. Presupposing the existence of math, which we should not do. Are you considering both genders? Only humans? What are your parameters?"

He fell back onto the bed. "Of course, we must consider the non-human element."

"It's a fair question," she said. She drifted back in and next to him. "Vampire, goblin, elf. And satyrs, of course. Werewolves, too. They're all viable."

She ran the back of her hand down his hairless chest. He was warm.

"Faery?" he asked.

"Oh, yes. It was their realm I left before coming here."

"Of course," he laughed. Then he gasped as her hand found its way down past his waist.

"And incubi and succubi," she said.

"Angels and demons?"

"Never a demon. They're repulsive. Even their women think so. And I've never met an angel."

"I think you might *be* one," he said.

She climbed up on her knees and straddled him.

"I've been a god," she said. "But never an angel."

She lowered herself down and let him in. It was time for another round.

~

"So you aren't an angel," he said later. Much later.

The sun had taken its leave entirely. They hadn't bothered to turn on any lights in the bedroom, but between the stray lamplight from the street and what was coming in through the doorway to the living room, there was no need.

They had eaten. On the kitchen counter was food ostensibly of Chinese origin in cardboard boxes. Eve had an intimacy with most regional foods, and considered the appropriate source region for this cuisine to be America. It might have been cooked by the Chinese, using techniques from East Asia, but the ingredients were too distinctly local for it to pass as authentic.

It also tasted better than the authentic version.

"I'm not an angel, no," she said.

She was sitting in a folding chair on his porch. The night had cooled, so she wore some clothes, and was wrapped in a light blanket. He was sitting in another chair, in the clothes he'd put on when he answered the door for the food.

"I doubt angels are real. I've not met one, which makes their existence unlikely."

"But demons are real? And faeries, and succubi and vampires and all that?"

He said it in a lightly mocking sing-song. He was treating this like a joke, which seemed an appropriate response under the circumstances. Most people didn't take well to the idea that there were other creatures living right next to them that they never saw, or saw but never noticed.

"Of course."

"Okay. If you say so."

"Their existence doesn't rely upon my testimony, Rick. They exist independent of my opinion."

He smiled. He had a shy smile. She enjoyed seeing it. "But your opinion *is* adequate on the matter of angels. And look, now I'm talking like you."

"It is, because angels are different. I can only testify that I've never encountered them. It's true, this doesn't negate their existence, but it makes their existence less likely. However, I have met these other creatures on many occasions. I don't *suppose* they exist. They simply do exist."

"I've never seen an angel either, since you're not one and you were my best candidate. But since I've never seen any of those other things either, it seems like they're on equal footing. Why does your not seeing an angel make it so unlikely that they're real? Mind you, I'm pretty sure *this* is the most ridiculous conversation I've ever had. You keep raising the bar."

"The reason my opinion is weightier is that I've witnessed the entirety of humankind. If an angel walked the Earth, I expect we'd have met."

He laughed. "And you've raised it some more."

When he saw she wasn't laughing, he sobered up.

"You're serious," he said.

"I am. And if your next question is, what could that possibly make me, if I'm not an angel or a god? The answer is the same as what I said before: many have considered me a god, and probably a few have thought of me as an angel. I'm neither, if those positions are defined by any kind of supernormal magical power. True magic of that kind doesn't exist, but I can do things that may appear magic to someone slightly more tethered to their mortality. I'm a woman, and that's all. What may make me different from the next woman is that it's possible I'm the very first one."

She had no reason to tell him this except that he had asked and she had grown tired of shunting his questions to the side or providing half-answers. And he was starting to take her seriously. No more laughter, no smile, nothing visibly indicative of a skepticism she was certain was there. His reaction was that of a person who'd just discovered a companion to be non-threateningly insane. Again, it was a appropriate response given the circumstance.

Eve had told many people a version of her life story on a thousand different occasions. The last time had been some fifteen years prior, to a young girl of whom she was fond. That girl decided to create something that might have been a religion had it happened a few hundred years earlier, and the consequence of her adoration was that many women in many corners of the world started calling Eve the *all-mother*. It was something she became less and less comfortable with over the years, so she stopped supporting the endeavor. In her last contact with one of the members—not the founder—she asked that the website and the organization beneath it be dismantled. Eve wasn't remotely competent enough to verify that this had happened.

"You understand how crazy that sounds?"

"I can't help that. The truth is what it is."

"Yeah, all right."

He got out of the chair and paced his way to the railing. He still moved like a coiled animal, even when on his elbows on a wood rail, leaning out over the spit of land beneath them. There was a sense that if he saw prey he would snag it out of the air.

"I feel like I should be asking for some kind of proof here," he said. "I mean, okay. You turned up out of nowhere in my coffee shop looking… like you do, and you're, you know, you're probably the most beautiful woman I've ever seen. And I'm saying that *after* all of that sex, so it's not just a line. But your clothes are all new, you've got a bag full of cash, and you talk like someone who's not just recent to the country. You sound like someone who climbed out of a space ship, or crawled out of a cocoon in some lab. Where did the cash even come from?"

"I knew I was going to need it to start. Before I found employment."

"Yeah, but that isn't answering the question. Everyone *needs* money, people don't just *get* it because they need it."

"Yes, I suppose this is true. I found it in one of the banks."

"You stole it."

"It didn't belong to me, and I took it, yes. I could speak at length on the notion of ownership and possession and how artificial I find intra-tribal commerce, but it may suffice for now to say I felt no moral qualms when I did this."

"*How* did you do it?"

"Through the veil. Solid things aren't as solid there."

He sighed grandly. "You can walk through walls?"

"Yes."

"Can you show me?"

"I could. I'm trying not to."

"I think you better explain that. I mean, I don't even get why you want a job if you can walk through bank walls and don't see anything wrong with it."

Her expression must have soured at the question, only because thinking about a response brought back unpleasant memories.

"I'm sorry, did I hit a nerve?" he asked.

"It's all right, I'll answer. It was pointed out to me recently that my disgust for so much of this world may come in part from my… detachment. The problem with traveling on the other side of the veil—which is what you've asked me to show you as proof —is when I do it I will leave you here. I'll remove myself, even if it's only a tiny bit and for the briefest of times. I'll be detached. There's a comfort to being there. I miss it, but I'm trying to wean myself."

"Someone said that to you? The disgust part."

"In so many words. My disgust was self-evident, and perhaps my detachment as well. He wasn't—he isn't a good man, the one who said this to me. Not good, but he has some wisdom. And I'm not a good woman. I was there to commit a murder."

"You know, every time I feel like we're settling down you bring out some new kind of crazy."

She laughed. "There's a long explanation."

"Did you do it?"

"No."

"That's good."

"I had been meaning to for a long time. It's… as I said, there is a long explanation, but I had… it was someone he cared about and I wanted him to suffer, and I thought I had found a way to *make* him suffer in the same way he made… I wanted him to suffer, and this was a poetically appropriate way. But I couldn't do it. And he knew, in the end, that I couldn't, so it didn't even serve that small purpose. He didn't know the kind of terror he *could* have known had there been truth behind my threat. He wasn't going to feel that loss of control over the life of a loved one at my hand. As soon as I realized that, I knew there was going to be no way of getting from him what I wanted."

"You wanted vengeance?"

"Yes, that's very close to right. But the enormity of the task… it would have given me none of what I wanted, and turned me into someone I didn't want to be any more. So I didn't do it. Millennia of waiting for such a moment, and I didn't do it."

She smiled grimly. "And now I'm here, trying to figure out who I'd like to be instead."

Rick smiled back. "That's quite an existential crisis you've got going on there."

"I suppose it is."

"I'm pretty sure I don't believe any of it. Only thing holding me back here is there's nothing at all about you that makes any sense, so if we're going with things that are crazy sounding, what you just said isn't so bad. Pretty sure I'd be saying the same thing about the spaceship idea or the cocoon thing."

"Or an angel."

"Or that. No wings, though."

She laughed. "I do know a thing with wings."

"Me too, we call them birds around here."

"Not a bird. A different thing."

She uncurled from the chair and stood at the edge of the balcony. They had passed a copse of trees on their way to the apartment earlier in the day, so there was a chance…

She made a series of low trills. There was a very specific note and cadence she was attempting, to issue a sound she'd not tried to issue for many years.

"What are you doing?" he asked.

"Shh."

She continued. He watched in silence, amused, confused or concerned, or all three. After about a minute, she heard a response, and then something flew past her line of vision.

"What was that?" Rick said.

"Did you see?" Eve asked.

"I don't know what I saw. Was that a bat?"

"No."

It flew past them again. Eve held out her arm in a pose more reminiscent of a falconer. It landed on her wrist.

"Hello, little one," she said.

"Oh my god, what?" Rick said. He edged closer. "What is that?"

"A pixie."

"She looks like… Tinkerbell. But with no clothes on."

Eve didn't know what a *Tinkerbell* was, but imagined the description was likely accurate. Pixies were tiny, flying creatures with gossamer wings and bodies that looked human. They didn't wear clothes, for the same reason most creatures don't wear clothes.

"Can we call you a *she*, little one?"

"Uh-huh," the pixie said.

Rick jumped back about three paces.

"Holy shit, she talks."

"Of course, they all can. Although not often and not well. They have their own language, which is what I was speaking earlier when I asked her to join us. I'm not fluent in their tongue but I have some words. No doubt I sound as simple to them in their language as they do to us in ours."

"How did… I don't…"

"Maybe you should sit down, Rick."

"Yes, okay."

He sat in the chair. It took a couple of tries because the chair was not perfectly aligned with his rear, and he couldn't seem to remove his eyes from the pixie.

"They tend to appear as female to us," Eve said. "But they are each both male and female. Some identify as male, and so I asked. You understand."

"No. Yes, sure. No."

To the pixie she asked, "What can I call you?"

"Dee," the pixie said.

"Hello, Dee."

"Hi." She flew off Eve's arm, circled Rick's head twice, and returned to the arm.

"He sick," she said.

"No, he's not sick. He's only confused."

"Uh-huh."

"Rick? I think Dee is hungry, do we have something we can give her?"

"Um…? What does she eat?"

"They eat insects, mostly, but have a fondness for certain fruits and fungi. Things that grow on or near trees."

"We have some *kung pao* left. Would she eat that?"

~

*D*ee didn't have any interest in *kung pao*, or in three of the other dishes provided. (Something with noodles and chicken, something with beef and a red sauce, something involving shrimp. Rick ordered enough food for a month, as far as Eve could discern.) Dee did take a liking to the mushrooms that accompanied a stir-fry dish, and seemed to enjoy the white rice. Rick also had an apple in his refrigerator that Dee started eating as soon as it warmed to room temperature.

They sat in the kitchen at the table and watched their new friend eat. Pixies could eat twice their weight in hardly any time at all.

Rick remained utterly flummoxed by the entire thing.

"I was prepared to accept that the stuff you were telling me was real *as far as you were concerned*," he said. "You know, because we all have our own… reality, I guess. Dated a witch once."

"Witches aren't real."

"Fair enough, but she thought she was. Like, not wiccan, or I guess not *just* wiccan. She thought she could make spells and do things, right? And it was fine. We'd be hanging out and something would happen, like, a little thing, something good. Find money on the ground, or make the bus on time, or something like that. And she'd be taking credit for it. I'd be like, *hey, I got a decent bonus* and she'd tell me she already knew because she brewed some special tea and set a chestnut on fire or something crazy. And I mostly just accepted that this was how the world worked for her. Didn't mean I had to accept it too."

"You're under no obligation to accept anything I say."

"Well yeah, but…" He gestured wordlessly to Dee. "Don't think I can pretend this isn't happening here."

Eve rubbed Dee's head. The pixie cooed gently, while continuing to eat.

"It's been my experience that people are as capable of denying things they experience directly as they are with things they're only told about. The perspective of humankind is extremely fragile. You're hardly the first person to see a pixie, and I've no doubt you know at least a goblin or an elf. Others are more rare or more regionally common, but all of this is to say you have run across a person or two who was only *somewhat* human. You only never knew it before now."

Dee finished eating, and took flight. She circled the room several times—it was impossible to say how many circuits only because pixies in flight are typically too quick for the eye—and then landed on Eve's shoulder.

"Doesn't she have to wait a half hour after eating or something?" Rick asked.

"You come see see now," the pixie said to Eve.

"Come see what, child?" Eve asked.

"Come see see."

"I'm sorry, I don't understand."

"See sick. Come see see, see sick."

"I still…" Eve looked at Rick, who was nodding.

"Cee, like the letter," Rick said. "I get it. Cee is a person, like Dee is. Or a pixie. A pixie person."

"Yes, Cee like Dee," Dee said. "But Cee sick, Dee not sick."

"Hello," Rick said.

He held out his hand, the way Eve had, and soon Dee was perched on him. Eve's heart broke a little at the idea of this confused man embracing the new strangeness of his world so much more openly than most of those who preceded him.

"Your friend Cee is a pixie like you?" he asked.

"Uh-huh. Cee sick."

"Do you want us to bring her food?"

"Uh-huh."

"All right, we can do that. Where is she?"

"In the tree."

"Which tree?"

"Big tree."

Rick looked up at Eve. "Any chance we get better directions?"

"No, but she can lead us there. It's probably not far."

"Not far," Dee said. "We fly. Very fast."

"We can't fly, little one," Eve said.

"Oh. Take longer then."

*H*umanity had developed a strong reliance on timekeeping. It was one of the things she found most curious about the modern world. Everyone had a watch or another device to track hours, minutes and seconds, and they all agreed that a certain time of day was always that time of day. In America, sometimes, everybody decided to ignore an hour, or add an extra hour, for no obvious reason. And there appeared to be a willful ignorance of the circularity of the globe. Five o'clock simply *was*, somehow.

According to Rick's cellular phone it was past ten PM when he and Eve and Dee left his home to wander the neighborhood in search of the big tree with the unhealthy pixie. Eve thought this was probably "late", but didn't expect to accustom herself to the regional diurnal schedule soon. She'd napped in between their sexual forays and had eaten a full meal, so this seemed like the ideal time to travel somewhere on foot. It was quickly apparent that she was the only one in the area who felt this way.

"The streets are so empty," she said.

"Dunno what you mean," Rick said. Two cars were just then driving past, making his point.

"I mean people, not cars."

"There's people *in* the cars. You know that, right? We don't have to have that conversation?"

"I realize they're machines being operated by people. I mean only that no one is sharing the sidewalk with us."

"This time of night, people are where they want to be or far enough away that they have to drive. Plus, it's Sunday. Do they have calendars where you're from?"

"No. And time moves much more quickly. This day has been eternal."

"Hope that's not a complaint."

"It isn't."

"Where did she go?"

With only the streetlights and a waning moon to see by, Eve was quickly developing an appreciation for more comprehensive footwear choices than what she currently had. The combination of sandals and bare feet was perfectly adequate in moderate climates for very nearly all of history, but didn't quite suffice in a modern urban landscape. Not when it was dark and the sidewalk was uneven.

They were going slowly, then, because she didn't dare walk much faster. Rick had to slow to her pace, as each of his strides was a stride-and-a-half of hers. The fast-moving pixie they were attempting to follow wasn't as courteous.

"She should be ahead," Eve guessed. She had no more idea than he, but they were approaching the same trees they'd passed earlier, which were in the approximate direction Dee had headed from the front door.

Rick was carrying a box of Chinese food in one hand and trying to keep his hand out to help Eve with the other. For the second time in the day, she considered how much faster it would be if he just tossed her over his shoulder.

"You know, this whole idea made a lot more sense inside. Now I'm just taking my leftovers for a walk."

They both picked up a familiar buzz. Dee hovered in front of Rick's face.

"You should learn to fly," she said. "Much faster."

"You're not wrong, little lady."

She humphed and flew off. Based on her departure trajectory, they appeared to be traveling in the correct direction.

"You think she's mad I called her little lady?" he asked. "It's kind of old-school sexist. Didn't mean it like that, it just came out."

"Pixies are mostly literal when they speak in the common tongue, so I doubt it. They have metaphors in their own, but I've never been able to understand their meanings. I think she likes you."

"Cool. Think she'll let me call her Tinkerbell?"

"You can ask. Pixies tend to prefer shorter names."

"Well I was joking anyway. Says her name's Dee, I'll call her that."

"Maybe she'll let you adopt her after I've left."

He laughed. "Number one, I didn't know that was a thing, so thank you, maybe I will. Number two, who said you're going anywhere?"

"This feels like the wrong place to have this conversation," she said.

"Why, because my neighbors can hear us? Look, I know what this is, but I also know you don't have another place to go right now, or a job, or more than three days of clothing, so I'm saying you can stick around."

Eve thought of all the ways she could respond, but nothing sounded both honest and kind, so she kept her silence. It was all right, because they'd reached the trees.

It was the sort of place that passed as a park for a heavily populated area, but it was really nothing more than a half-dozen trees, a curated lawn, and two wood benches. It was comically inadequate.

"I know this isn't true," she said, "but if you told me this was the last evidence of a continental forest, I might believe you."

"Nah, this is new. Used to be a public lot, they decided to put the trees in a couple years ago. It's not a forest, but it's not nothing."

"No. But it's close to nothing. I don't know if you know what a forest really is."

"Yeah, kids these days, don't even know what a real forest is."

"Are you making fun of me?"

"A little bit, yeah."

Dee returned.

"Big tree!"

She buzzed around their heads until they made it off the sidewalk, down the manicured lawn, and to the third of six trees. It didn't look particularly large in comparison to the rest. It was tall, but they were all tall.

"Okay, we're here, Dee," Rick said. "Where's your friend?"

"Top," Dee said.

Rick had a function on his cellular phone that turned it into a flashlight, which he used to assess the height of the tree.

"Oh dear," he said. "Been a long time since I climbed a tree."

"I'll do it," Eve said.

"No, no, I can do it, I'm just figuring out the best way to start."

"I used to have to scale trees much larger and less accommodating, with a predator bearing down. I promise, I am a better climber than you."

He turned the light on her.

"We're really doing this? The whole *older than mankind* thing, we're sticking with that story?"

"It's my life story. I only have one."

"Right. Okay, sure. How can I help?"

"You can save us time by lifting me to that lower bough, and keeping the light trained on the upper branches."

"Fine."

He seemed put out to be ceding the tree duties to her. She imagined it was some artifact of chivalry he was answering to. But it didn't make sense for him to risk his own health at something she could perform more efficiently, especially for a tree this small. His weight might bring down a branch that could support her.

She kicked off her sandals. He put his hands under her arms. "Okay, we'll do this like a dance move, right? Count of three, I'll lift you over my head."

A three-count, and then he essentially threw her straight up. She had no trouble grabbing hold of the lowermost narrow limb, and in fact nearly missed it because she overshot slightly. The tree complained with a tiny crackling sound, but otherwise held her.

She swung up and onto the branch, then began feeling her way higher, the familiar sense of bark between her toes and—in spots where there was no branch strong enough—between her thighs.

We came from the trees, she thought. *To the trees we always return.*

Dee buzzed by her ear at a little more than halfway up.

"How close are we?"

"Higher," she said. "Almost."

It didn't occur to Eve until she had nearly reached the highest point that what she was doing made no sense. She'd never known a pixie to get sick, so what was probably happening was that Dee's friend Cee was expiring from old age, not suffering from some kind of ailment. That being the case, there wasn't anything Eve, or Rick, or anyone could do aside from bury her politely once she was gone. Food wasn't going to help.

"Is she too weak to fly?" Eve asked.

"Too weak."

You could have carried her down, she thought.

That was the other part of why what Eve was doing didn't

make sense. Pixies could carry things heavier than other pixies. There was no reason Dee couldn't have brought her friend to the base of the tree.

"How are you doing?" Rick asked.

"I think I'm almost there."

"Okay. You want me to throw the food to you or something?"

"I'll bring her down."

"Okay. So you know, watching you climb a tree is maybe the sexiest thing I've seen all day."

"Thank you."

"You're welcome. Also, someone just walked by and probably thought I was saying that to a squirrel, so I appreciate you answering."

She laughed.

The nest was in a Y-shaped split near the very top. It was made of leaves from the tree, and woven twigs. In many ways it looked no different than a bird's nest, but there was a complexity in the detail that indicated this was something crafted by a being with fingers and thumbs.

Inside the nest was a brown-haired pixie.

"Hello," Eve said. "You must be Cee."

Cee didn't speak. She moved her little head in recognition of having been spoken to, but that was all.

There was definitely something wrong with Cee.

Eve had seen pixies die of old age on several occasions. It was sad, but rather dignified. Mostly, they put their heads down and went to sleep and didn't ever wake up again.

Whatever was happening to Cee wasn't at all like that. She looked like she was trapped in a spider's web, but there was no spider.

"Child, where have you been flying?"

～

Taking Cee down took some time. Before seeing the pixie's condition Eve thought it might be possible to slip her into a pocket prior to descending, but as soon as she laid eyes on the poor thing she knew that wasn't going to work. Cee was in a fragile condition, and she was also attached to the nest somehow. So instead, Eve took the entire nest with her and descended one-handed.

"Here, hand it down," Rick said when she was within arm's reach.

"I don't want you to touch her," she said.

"I won't hurt her."

"That isn't my concern."

She and the nest jumped down together instead, sort-of caught by Rick before hitting the ground.

"How is she?" he asked. "Should we give her the food?"

"Not here. We have to bring her back. I need better light."

"Something's wrong," he guessed.

"I think so."

A short walk later, Cee and the nest were resting on the little-used dining table in Rick's home. Dee was flying around Rick's head at an unseemly velocity—an indication of worry.

"I take it this isn't what they look like when they die," he said. He was leaning too close.

"Please, don't touch her," Eve said.

"Yeah, I get that. I won't hurt her."

"My concern is for you. She's sick, but I don't know what with."

Cee appeared to be melting. No other description seemed fully adequate to the task. The web it looked like she was caught in was part of her body, and it was sticky. She was adhered to the nest.

"You're worried I'm gonna catch whatever this is? What about you?"

"I don't respond to diseases," she said. "I never have."

He laughed. "Sure, okay. Makes sense. Must be nice."

Eve touched the stringy part of Cee with the end of a pencil. Something *did* seem a little familiar about this. She'd never witnessed a pixie melt—ostensibly because pixies didn't melt—but maybe she'd seen it happen to something else.

"It's not at all nice," she said. "I've seen every plague this world ever imagined and every manner of deliberate suffering conceivable. Knowing it would not befall me doesn't mean I had no direct participation in the ensuing suffering, only that it didn't end my life as well. On many occasions I wished it had."

"Cee sick," Dee said, buzzing past Eve's ear. The pixie was little more than a rush of wind with a voice.

"I agree, child. But of what I don't know."

"You've seen every plague in history," Rick said, "and you don't recognize this one?"

"No, which is why you should stand away."

"Maybe you don't understand how germs work. If that's contagious enough, you brought it in the condo and put it on my table. I may already be exposed."

"I appreciate your point, but you told me you never eat at this table."

"Not really what I meant."

It was almost elastic, the string leading from Cee. Pulling on it didn't cause her any visible pain, but she was close to passing and may not have been positioned to offer comprehensive feedback.

Eve put the pencil down.

"I know what you meant, Rick. I understand that some sicknesses can pass through the air and others require touch. A few are only passed if one eats the thing that is sick."

"No eat!" Dee said.

"We aren't going to eat your friend, Dee."

"Okay."

"Pixies can fly anywhere. If Cee could receive and further

transmit this sickness through the air, you would hardly be the only human victim. However she contracted this, she isn't communicating it so easily."

"But you don't want me to touch her."

"An unreasonable risk you don't need to take."

"Right. So I won't touch."

He sat down at the table to get a closer look. Dee stopped flying to sit on his shoulder.

"And you've never seen anything like this?" he asked.

"I didn't say that. I have never seen this happen as the consequence of a disease, yes." She began probing Cee with her finger, gently. The poor thing was sticky all over.

"Right, because if there was some sort of Wicked Witch of the West virus out there I bet you wouldn't forget."

"What did you call it?"

"Like in *The Wizard of Oz*? The movie."

She knew what movies were, and television shows, and the Internet. She didn't watch them, for the most part, but she knew what they were. This was a reference that escaped her.

"The witch melts," he said with a light laugh. "Dorothy throws water on the wicked witch and she melts. I guess that's not so funny, really, cuz… cuz this must suck for her. But that's what I meant."

"I understand," Eve said.

Cee was exuding some sort of oil, and the horrible possibility that the oil was her liquefying body couldn't be ignored.

She got up from the table to wash her hands in the sink.

"Cee eat," Dee said.

"I don't know if food's gonna do it," Rick said.

Eve toweled off and retrieved the food they'd carried all the way to the park and back. She extracted a bit of mushroom from the container.

"How do *you* feel, Dee?" she asked.

"I worry," the pixie said.

"Yes, but do you feel sick too?"

"No."

Eve held the mushroom next to Cee's mouth. There was no response aside from a tiny eye-roll.

"I'm sorry Dee," Eve said, "I think she doesn't have long to live."

Dee's response was to start flying around the room again.

"Some kind of acid, maybe?" Rick suggested.

"No. We found her in her own nest. Whatever she was exposed to, she was well enough to fly home before it took effect. I imagine the water thrown on this witch you were speaking of had an immediate impact as well."

"Yeah. And there was smoke and lots of cackling."

Eve didn't entirely understand movies, but thought that perhaps the reason this was so had more to do with her unique perspective than on the quality of cinematic entertainment. Watching events transpire from a safe remove was what she had spent an immodest amount of her own life doing. Entertainment was a temporary escape from reality, but in this case the appeal of a movie *was* her reality.

"That sounds awful," Eve said.

"Yeah, but you know. She was the villain."

"How much easier that must be, to know whose death to mourn and whose to celebrate."

He did that thing he did when he was uncomfortable, rubbing the back of his neck and very nearly blushing. "I wasn't looking to start a philosophical conversation, Eve. It's just a movie."

"I understand," she said. "The witch represents a threat to your tribe and so her defeat is a cause for celebration. She is portrayed as disfigured and something other than human, and so you see her as an objective danger. This is the ideological foundation on which every war in history was fought. I don't need that explained to me."

"Jesus," he muttered.

"Yes," she said. "His story followed that pattern as well, only in that tale *he* was the witch."

"No, I mean… it was an epithet, not a subject. I just didn't really get how much baggage someone your age is carrying around. And I say that as someone who is still pretty sure he doesn't believe you."

"You mean metaphorically. Baggage."

"Yeah yeah."

She sat back down in front of the suffering pixie. In a moment she was going to have to make the difficult decision of ending this poor thing's life, because Cee was not going to get better and there was no telling how much worse she would become. But for the moment all Eve could think about was that very first war.

It wasn't correct, thinking of it that way. There had always been early groups, or tribes, wandering communities of humankind that had cohered based upon familial relation or social/regional commonality, or something even more trivial. These tribes would rub up against one another and either combine or compete, and when they competed it was a war.

Those wars weren't real to her, back then. They were petty conflicts that happened to the less advanced, to people she barely even thought of as *like* her and hers. They were *others*. But then those others became an army, and then there was a real war. In her mind, that was the first.

She and hers lost that war.

"I'm sorry for my baggage," she said. "But you've made me think."

"About witches?"

"About war. Cee's condition isn't entirely unfamiliar. You remember I spoke of demons before?"

"I do. Seems like a long time ago now."

"Demons are huge beasts. They are perpetually angry, blood-thirsty, violent creatures that can't be reasoned with, and some are also quite shrewd. They are one of the most dangerous species on Earth."

"Cool. I'll keep an eye out."

"They are the consummate warrior, and make ideal vanguard soldiers. But they have a weakness. Their bodies are unusually corruptible."

"How's that?"

"They become sick easily. And in death—through any means —they will dissolve. They melt, as your witch does when exposed to water."

"So, I just learned about pixies a few hours ago, but I'm gonna guess they're not related to demons."

"No. And this is not how a pixie dies. More, demons don't melt and then die, they die and then melt. But, it's similar. How the two relate is not something I understand right now."

She stroked the side of Cee's head. The pixie was still responsive, but just barely.

"She can't tell us where she's been or how this happened to her. And she's suffering. Dee?"

Dee buzzed next to her head. "Yes. Can you fix?"

"I can't fix, no. I'm sorry. But I can help her go peacefully. You should say goodbye."

~

*C*ee was executed as painlessly as they could manage, using a knife and a cutting board. They buried the pixie in an unused garden bed in the yard beneath his porch, and threw both the cutting board and the knife in the trash. Dee buzzed inconsolably and then flew away to mourn more substantively in private.

Later, they slept, and Eve dreamed.

She wasn't used to the experience. She didn't sleep often in the faery realm—for whatever reason, there was little need—but when it came, it didn't bring along any dreams.

It was a nightmare, in truth. It had been even longer since she'd experienced one of those.

In the dream, the faces of many of the people she loved were right in front of her, but she couldn't talk to them, or touch them, and they couldn't see her. They were on the other side of a screen, in a movie or on the wrong end of the veil. They couldn't hear her. They didn't know she was there.

This was terrible enough, but worse when they began to melt like so much candle wax.

And then *he* was there.

He had many names. Urr was the oldest she knew him by, but Adam was what he called himself currently. It was a poorly chosen name: Cain, from the same source material, would have been as accurate and more suitable.

Adam *could* see and hear her, and also them, and he had the power to help her friends. She didn't know how or why this was so, only that it was. And he wouldn't do it.

A young girl named Aia grabbed his arm and begged for assistance. Aia was a Gaulish woman Eve remembered with great affection from a time before France was France. She was a beautiful peasant maiden felled too young by consumption. Now half her face was sliding from her skull with her tears.

Adam laughed, and pushed Aia away. She fell in a heap at his feet. The affront was so horrific, Alfarr—an elvin warrior whose name actually meant *elf warrior*—charged Adam, wielding a broadsword. Alfarr had been one of Eve's favorite lovers. Seeing him disintegrate completely before reaching his target caused her to scream.

Still, Adam laughed. He picked up the unused sword and began swinging it about the room, taking the heads of those who still had them.

Eve slapped at the screen separating her from the world, but couldn't get through. She could only watch, and she couldn't stop watching.

"They're all the same," Adam said. "Don't you see?" Then he swung the sword at the veil, tearing it open.

"We are the same too," he said, stepping through. He raised the sword to strike her down.

She awoke with what must have been a shout.

"Hey, you okay?"

Rick poked his head into the bedroom. He was fully clothed, in a collared shirt and slacks, and had a necktie on, loosely.

"Yes, I am, thank you." It was morning, as the east-facing porch doors betrayed. She blinked and tried to recall where she was and why. "Hello."

"Hello to you. I was gonna let you sleep. Left a note out here and everything, but… so you're awake and I can just tell you. There's a spare key next to the note so you can get in and out all you want."

"A key."

"Yes, you know. This is how people who can't walk through walls get by. We have doors with keys and such. Also, please remember that when you leave we lock doors, like, all the time."

"Oh. Thank you. Where are you going?"

"It's Monday?"

She shook her head. Something about Monday was important, but an explanation wasn't coming. She was still living out the dream and wondering when Rick's face was going to start melting.

"I have to go to work," he explained. "That's what we do on this plane of existence or whatever. Are you going to be here when I get home?"

"I don't know."

He nodded. "It is what it is. For the record, I'd rather you were here and I hope you stay."

"I enjoy your company as well."

"Good to hear. Oh, also, your pixie came back this morning. She keeps hanging around me. Followed me into the bathroom. That was weird."

"I believe she is more your pixie than mine, Rick."

"Super. Can't wait to explain that one to the boss. Okay, I'm late. Like I said, hope you're here later."

"I… yes. Yes, I hope I am too."

"Then it's an almost-date-thing. Bye."

He left with no kiss or hug or other manifest display of affection, which only meant he understood her well. The truth was, she had no idea if she would be there either. Asking for a promise would have been a mistake.

They're all the same.

Dream-Adam's voice still echoed in her skull. There was some truth buried in that sentiment. She was going to have to figure out what it was.

FOUR

here was so much she had forgotten.

It was difficult to explain what it was like to *be* on the other side of what she called the veil. To begin with, the very definition—while descriptive—wasn't accurate. Going there wasn't like pulling aside a curtain (or cutting it with a sword) and stepping through so much as it was traveling in an entirely new direction. Putting that into words was a little like trying to explain *up* to someone who only knew left-right and forward-back, so instead she used terminology that was more at home in legend and mysticism.

Traveling the Earth while using this new direction was simple, and fast because time and space were much more flexible. In the veil, to get to where she wanted to be, she could walk, and jump, and be there in an instant of veil-time.

In the world *outside* the veil, she had to take a bus.

It was unpleasant. The bus moved in fits and starts and spat out black clouds so routinely it had to be an indication of its proper function rather than a grievous manufacturing error. The best that could be said was that it was not full; the rush of the morning commute had already passed by the time Eve got out of bed and showered and put on clothing.

As to where she was taking the bus, she didn't know. Had the events of the prior evening never taken place Eve imagined she would be looking into what was needed in order to obtain a job. This had been the original plan, but it was making less sense the longer she considered it. To have a job she needed a name, and a document showing that the name wasn't one she'd just made up. There had to be numbers attached to that name, and those numbers had to have a validity that made them impossible to invent. Without those things, she didn't know how she was going to find a job.

Not, it had to be said, that she *wanted* a job. What she wanted was to immerse herself in this world for at least long enough to appreciate it as something to not despise, the way *he* appreciated it.

For too long she'd treated the world—the entire thing—as his tribe. She visited, but didn't join. She didn't *want* to join, but there were no other tribes from which to choose, and she needed to belong somewhere again.

The plan made more sense in general terms. The specifics were a good deal more complicated.

The bus would eventually stop in a downtown hub. She hadn't concerned herself with which hub or what town. City buses returned to cities when they were done with their circuits, and that was all she needed to know for the moment. It was what she would have done in seeking out a job, or the paperwork for one, and what she was still doing in order to figure out why she had to mercy kill a pixie on a cutting board.

As goals, neither task seemed attainable, but at least with the pixie problem she had something that seemed close to a plan.

∾

The bus did indeed arrive at a downtown destination, full of achingly tall buildings and uncomfortably over-dressed people. She got out and wandered around until finding a bench near an active central spot—an outdoor market. Then she sat down and began watching as the whole of humanity hurried past.

She had a tremendous amount of experience watching people, but less experience being seen doing it, so she had to keep reminding herself not to actively stare at the passers-by.

It was difficult.

So much about a person could be discovered in a close observation of the sort that simply wasn't polite in most public circumstances. For instance, there was the obese man in a cavernous jacket and white shirt, with suspenders keeping his pants up. The suspenders stretched to the left and right of his gut. He had wire-rim glasses and a large nose, and sweat stains on his collar. His walk was bow-legged, as if he'd just climbed off a horse.

He looked like someone who should be miserable, but underneath all the external trappings of excess and self-evident physical limitations, he twinkled with a happiness that suggested he was using a different set of measuring scales than she was. She wanted to understand why, but to do so would be to intrude on his life in a way that was unforgivably bold.

Five teenaged girls pushed past the man. They were dressed in shorts and comfortable shoes, and short-sleeve blouses with a hint of fashionable distinction. They were too thin and too tall for their own bodies. Puberty was making them awkward and giggly, horribly insecure separately but operating as a unit with a pooled confidence that made it all okay. Eve wished she could follow them too, to see how their dynamic played out and what choices they made and what they deemed important collectively.

But that wasn't why she was there.

Amidst the hundreds of people rushing past one another in the market, there were other beings. It was a secret thing, only she never remembered it was a secret; she could see them clearly enough. They were easy to spot, and they were almost the reason she was there.

The marketplace was an open cobblestone pavilion with vendor carts set up in rows running alongside buildings containing more goods. The foot traffic was chaotic on a local scale, but there was a consistency to the flow around the carts. There was a current, essentially, and it picked up everyone. It moved quickly enough that the obese man never noticed the teenaged girls, and they never noticed the two older women with bags on their shoulders in slacks and heels and soft shirts stopping in front of a vendor of fresh pastries. The teens also didn't notice that one of the women was a goblin. Neither, Eve suspected, did the goblin's human companion.

Behind the goblin, in an alcove set off a distance from the main thoroughfare, a large man in a hooded jacket stepped onto the sidewalk, looked around for a particular individual he failed to locate, and then stepped back into the shadow. He was a demon. Nobody noticed him either, which was to everyone's benefit.

There would be more as the day went on. An hour after the goblin left with her friend and her meal, a man dressed in clothing that was historically anachronistic arrived at a meeting spot at the edge of the market. It was no small thing for his clothing to be so out-of-place that even Eve recognized it as being inappropriate for the period, so there was little question he stood out in the eyes of the crowd. People began to follow him around as he told incredible stories about the historical relevance of nearly every brick under their feet. The stories beggared belief, yet the man's storytelling prowess was such that it was hard to question any of it.

He was an imp, without any doubt.

She spotted another goblin toward the end of the day, and a pair of elves, and a man who may have been a werewolf. And when she decided to leave her bench and walk through some of the nearby stores she found an incubus selling shirts. She expected come nightfall, there would be a vampire or two, and no doubt one of the bars ringing the marketplace had an iffrit hiding within its recesses.

None of the beings she saw looked ill. There were numerous instances of human ailments on display, but nothing notable in the much smaller sampling of non-humans.

She heard a familiar buzzing as the sun began to set.

"Hello, Dee," she greeted. The pixie landed on her shoulder.

"'Lo."

"What are you doing here?"

"Man sent."

"Rick sent you?"

"Uh-huh."

Eve laughed. It didn't take long at all for Rick to figure out how useful a pixie could be, especially when trying to find someone.

"Did he give you a message?"

"Uh-huh."

A woman pushing a child in a wheeled device took note of Eve talking to her shoulder, but continued past. Eve hardly concerned herself with what other people thought, but was mindful of the merits of not causing a scene. She decided to relocate from the bench she'd claimed for much of the day to a secluded spot under a tree that the streetlights hadn't discovered.

"What is his message?"

"He cook."

"That's... all?"

"Uh-huh."

Eve had left behind her bag with most of her money and all of her clothes. She *did* take the key he'd left for her, and hoped it was self-evident that in doing so she had decided to return. It didn't make sense for him to send Dee just to notify her dinner was going to be ready soon.

"Are you sure you aren't forgetting anything?"

"Nope. Tell girl about cooking and give note and that's all."

"All right, so there's a note?"

"Yes, note," Dee said, with a hint of frustration in her voice. Pixies tended to think humans were just as stupid as humans thought of pixies. "Here."

She handed over a rolled-up piece of notepaper that, in the twilight and under the tree, Eve couldn't read. She stepped into a pool of lamplight.

It was his address. Or so she assumed. It was *an* address, at least.

"In case you lost," Dee said.

"Is that what he told you?"

"Uh-huh. Silly."

"Why is that silly?"

"You not lost, you right here."

"I am indeed." But as she looked around the market where she'd spent her day, she realized she couldn't recall the exact bus that had brought her. "The question is, where precisely is here?"

~

*R*ather than attempt to retrace her steps via public transit, Eve put the funds in her pocket to use and paid a taxi to get back to Rick's.

"There you are," he said, from the kitchen space. He was indeed cooking. He had an apron on—it looked so perfectly clean he surely dug it out of a drawer, or purchased it that day—and was standing over a vat atop the stove. "I'm making my famous pasta."

"You're known for your cuisine?" She took a seat at the dining table.

"Oh yes. I buy the very best canned sauce. Should be ready in a few. Did Dee find you?"

"She did. That was very clever."

"She offered. I think she's crushing on me."

"It's not uncommon," Eve said, not entirely clear on what *crushing* was but inferring the meaning from usage. "Why did you send me your address?"

He laughed. "Just in case. Did you need it?"

"I did. But how did you know I would?"

"I have family in Venezuela," he said. "Distant, you know, we're not close or anything, but one time I get this call from my dad letting me know I have a cousin who's gonna be visiting, and can he crash here? So I say yes, because, family and all. So this kid shows up, never been to the States before, and he's, like, saucer-eyed about the whole experience. Starts wandering around his first day without *any* idea where he's gonna end up. He gets so lost the police end up calling his family in Venezuela, who call my dad, who calls me, because the kid didn't even think to take *my* number with him and he couldn't remember my name or where I lived. So the second day he was here, I wrote my address out and my phone and made him keep it in his wallet. You don't have a phone, but once I saw you were planning on coming back I figured why not make sure you knew how to do that."

"Well it was very thoughtful."

"Yeah, plus I can't eat all this tortellini by myself. Hope you're hungry."

She was. At the market she'd purchased a meal constructed primarily out of animal fat and cooking oil. It was distressingly tasty, but she disliked the way it felt in her stomach. The consequence of remaining in this reality appeared to be a rediscovery of her appetite for many things, with a voraciousness that was perhaps not healthy.

"I would like to clean myself before your meal is ready," she said. "I have too much of the marketplace on me."

"The market, huh? You didn't bring home any bags."

"I wasn't shopping, I was looking for something."

"Didn't find it?"

"Not yet, but perhaps I will tomorrow."

"Cool. Well, this is gonna be ready in a minute. Want me to join you in that shower?"

She smiled. "Yes, I would."

Eve stood, took off her blouse, and left the room.

The pasta was not as tasty as the lunch from the market, but it sat better and left her with fewer regrets.

The sex was much improved.

This was not to say anything had been lacking in their first day together, but sex was something she'd always found to be more engaging when novelty and familiarity were balanced. They were reaching that point.

There were no notes from Rick the following morning releasing her from any expectation of being there at the end of the day. He left for work assuming she would be there when he got back.

She was.

Eve spent the day at the marketplace again, this time taking note of which buses to employ to complete the round-trip. She returned to the marketplace again the following day, and the day after, and another six days after that—including two days constituting the weekend, in which Rick did not have to appear at his employer's office. He went with her to the market instead, and gamely attempted to comprehend why they were sitting together on a bench and apparently just staring at people.

By the morning of the ninth day she was prepared to

surrender the quest and initiate the much more mundane task of seeking employment. So of course it was on that day she found what she was looking for.

It was an elf, and he had a cold.

Nearly all creatures could get sick. In one instance—demons —the acquisition of a disease was nearly always fatal, but in most it was dealt with in the same way as it was in humans. They suffered until they get better, or they didn't get better and, over time, they died.

The concept of immune systems was a medical one for which Eve only recently developed an understanding, because science moved faster than her attention to it. But she could draw a correlation between life expectancy and relative immunity.

Elves and goblins—they were actually the same species, but with different regional identifiers—lived about as long as humans, and so got sick roughly as frequently. Likewise satyrs. Incubi and succubi lived about twice as long (and looked twenty-five for most of their lives) so became ill less often. Imps lived longer still, got sick less, and so on.

Those were only the most obvious species, the ones that were common and could pass unnoticed fairly easily as human in the light of day. There were rarer things out there that she knew less about, and didn't care for an opportunity to improve upon that understanding. The rakshasa, for instance, she would just as soon not get to know better. Likewise the djinn, provided there still existed any.

The elf with the cold was dressed in slacks and a blazer, with a white shirt and tie. She'd spent enough time in the market by then to recognize the minor differences in formal clothes from man to man. There were suits where the fabric of the jacket and the pants matched in pattern, color and type. These were less common and more likely tailored to fit. The men who dressed like this also tended to have a crisper-looking shirt, a striped tie with a color in it that closely matched the suit, and a piece of metal in the tie to hold it to the shirt. They also had shinier shoes. Eve thought it was possible these more thoroughly formal outfits were indicators of status, but she couldn't be sure.

Much more popular was the dark pants and dark blazer, where the two didn't appear to have been purchased as a set. A range of shirt colors went with this pairing, the ties were often more haphazard and free-swinging, and there was, overall, a sort of ruffled quality to the wearers. The outfit still matched the uniform of the local business industry—whatever that business was—but had a more every-day sense to it. This arrangement of clothing could have also been linked to status, in the same way as the tailored suits.

Her impression of the elf was that he was not a member of the ruling class of bespoke suit-wearers, yet more important than the people who wore no suits at all. (Those people often had uniforms as well, but the kind indicating a position in the service industry.) He carried a white tissue in his hand and appeared either about to sneeze or just recovering from one. His eyes and nose were red-rimmed, which was all the more noticeable on a creature known for a light complexion.

As was true for everyone else in the market, the elf was in a hurry to get somewhere. Eve decided to follow.

It became apparent almost immediately that the elf knew he was being followed, due to some skill on his part, a lack of subtlety on hers, or a combination. His direct route to wherever he had intended to go—it was toward the office buildings so she presumed his destination was one of them—turned into an indirect meander. It wasn't until a trip down a side street became an evasive duck behind a dumpster and into an alley that Eve decided she had better exercise caution.

One must always assume, in dealing with an elf, that they have a knife on their person.

"Hello," she said, from the edge of the alley. The smell of

liquefied waste in the dumpster was hair-curling. "I didn't mean to alarm you, I only wanted to ask a question."

A long silence followed. She wondered if he had exited the other end of the alley and she was talking to an empty space. She also wondered if it would have been a better idea to have Dee with her.

"What is your question?" came his reply.

"May I enter?" she asked.

"With your hands out, yes."

She stepped past the dumpster, hands at her sides and palms out.

The elf was a third of the way down the alley, using what little shadow he could find. The knife she suspected him of carrying was in his left hand. His right held the tissue.

"I'm sorry to have worried you," she said.

He looked puzzled. "Do you dye your hair?"

"No."

"My eyes are watery and the sun's bright, but you look like kin, except for the hair."

"I am no kin to an elf."

"Human?"

"In a manner, yes."

"Come closer."

She approached, until they were only a few paces away. With his knife still exposed, he looked her up and down. She kept her hands where they were and did her level best to not appear threatening.

"What do you mean, *in a manner?*" he asked.

"I'm human, but I've been known by names of beings you would not consider human. An elf might know me as Iounn or Idunna. I've also been called the Way-Finder, and the Gardener."

He laughed. "I was a kid when I heard those stories. Is Zeus with you? He's running late, perhaps."

"No, Zeus is long dead," she said, entirely serious because it was true. The proto-Greek man whose stories later became married to the Zeus god-myth was long dead. "I thought most of your kind kept to the secret stories."

"You mean, we believed them?"

"That's what I mean, yes."

He shrugged. "I guess there are some that still do. A pretty redhead in an alley claiming to be a passel of ancient gods is a long way from that, though."

"Most people would say the same about a man claiming to be an elf."

He laughed, but the laugh quickly turned into a cough, which became bad enough to grab hold of his entire body. Soon, the knife was on the ground and he was leaning on Eve for support while waiting for the attack to subside.

"Thank you," he said quietly. "I'm glad you aren't here to mug me. I think I just gave you the opening you needed."

"No. Only a question, as I said." She bent down and retrieved his knife. He took it from her, hilt-first, and slid it into his sleeve.

"Go ahead."

"Who is your doctor?"

"I'm… sorry?"

"I assume you are seeing one?"

Elves and goblins could pass easily as humans in most arenas of life, but a medical exam wasn't one of those places. This was equally so for other species, and it led to a shadow medical industry few were aware of. If an elf were sick he would go to a doctor who treated elves. If he wanted his pointed teeth capped he would go to a dentist who specialized in *that* and so on, all the way down to schooling and matrimonial bonds and funeral arrangements.

"Do you need a doctor? I thought you said you were human, why don't you see one of theirs? They aren't rare."

"I don't need to see him for medical advice for myself, but I do have some questions I believe a medical expert in the more exotic species may be able to answer. Have you already sought treatment for your condition?"

"For this? I was there a few days ago. He gave me some pills. He said I should be better soon."

"So… he knew what you've contracted?"

"Sure, he called it… I forget. He did say to expect it to get worse before it gets better, but I should turn the corner by next week, if I keep up with the pills."

"I see."

There were questions she could have asked if she understood disease even a little better. There were different kinds—viral, bacterial—and there was cancer, and surely there were other types still. She would have liked to ask what the pills were supposed to be doing for him, and how. But she was certain even if he knew the answer she wouldn't understand it.

I'll ask the doctor instead.

"Can you provide me with a way to contact him?"

"Sure, I can give you his name. So this is for a friend?"

"Yes, exactly. It's for an associate of mine who was recently ill. I was looking for advice on helping them."

"Be easier if you just brought the friend."

"Yes, I might."

The elf pulled out his wallet and extracted a business card. "I always keep one or two extras with me. You never know when you're going to meet another one of our kind looking for a referral."

"Thank you," she said, taking the card. "And I hope you feel better soon."

"Thanks, I'm sure I will."

She sincerely hoped that was the case, because when she caught him during his coughing fit, she touched his skin.

It was sticky.

FIVE

"Tell me again why we're doing this?"

Rick was driving. The car they were using was borrowed from a service he subscribed to, via a process he attempted to explain but which she failed to fully grasp.

It seemed as if the world had developed indirect substitutes for money, which was confusing inasmuch as money was itself a substitute for goods. A car was a very real object, but he hadn't purchased the car, he'd bought time from the company that owned the car. Except that was also not accurate. He had bought a lump of time from the company, using an internet-based monetary instrument, which had a value that appeared to be unrelated to the value of a known currency, at least until the day he needed it to represent real currency, and then he could exchange it at whatever rate was current at that moment.

The acquisition of a lump of time struck Eve as a wholly ridiculous expenditure, as time was even less real than money, internet-based or not. Nonetheless, he was able to take a portion of this lump of time and transfer it to the company that owned the car, which gave him use of the car for roughly the same amount of time as the lump he'd given them. It was only approximately the same time lump, as there was something called *free minutes* involved, and that was when she gave up trying to understand.

"I just want to ask him some questions. I have never seen anything like this before."

"I know, but this doesn't seem so much like just curiosity any more. I mean, happy to do this with you, I just wanna make sure there isn't anything you aren't telling me, here."

They'd gone over this two or three times already. It was hard for her to put to words what she was feeling, so she had only supplied him with vague responses. The truth was she could still hear dream-Adam's voice, now coupled to a strong notion that there was something significantly amiss outside of that dream.

"It *is* more than curiosity. That is perhaps the wrong word."

It was late in a weekday, six days after the elf had given her the card, and the first time the doctor—his name was Lawrence Monks—could fit them into his schedule. She had returned to the marketplace each of those six days to see if there were any other sick non-humans to interrogate. There weren't, but she did see the sick elf two more times. He didn't look like he was getting any better, but the last time they spoke he promised he *felt* better, and was sure he was turning a corner.

She hoped this was true. But the same feeling she had so much trouble describing to Rick was also telling her that the elf had gotten worse, and that was the reason she hadn't seen him again.

"An instinct, then," he said. "A gut instinct."

"I suppose."

They were on a highway and traveling at a preposterous speed. It was late afternoon, so the road was heavily trafficked by people who had gone into the city to work in the morning and were now evacuating. Given the distances involved, the whole concept struck her as ridiculous. She knew of entire civilizations whose citizens never traveled as far in a lifetime as one commuter here might go in a day.

"I'll tell you how it feels," she said. "Imagine you enter your home one night. All the lights are off and you live alone. Something isn't right, but you can't figure out what, until you notice one end of your couch has been moved backwards by a hand's width. That's what it feels like."

"Okay. Okay, that's a start. Let's call that confusion and dread. And the world is your living room?"

"This world is someone else's responsibility. But I know where all of the furniture is. Metaphorically."

"Yeah, okay. And the rest of that story is, if I'm in my living room and my couch has been moved, and I didn't do it, maybe there's someone else in my living room."

"Yes."

"Got it."

The electronic woman in the car's front panel informed Rick that they were nearing their exit. Eve understood that the woman was a talking map, but that didn't make her comfort with this technology any more manageable. Maps used to have borders, and beyond those borders were exciting new lands. The woman's cold certainty couched in a United Kingdom accent only the map's borders had run out of monsters.

This could be why I'm chasing a vague feeling, she thought. *Something new.*

"I'm sorry," she said. "I shouldn't have involved you in something like this. I'm sure I am overreacting to a simple thing."

"Hey, no, this is fun!" he said, as they took the correct, clearly marked and fully expected highway exit. "I just wanted to make sure I understood all the pieces, in case you were, I don't know, forgetting to tell me anything."

"I don't believe I am, but I am unaccustomed to sharing information as well, so… I apologize if I seem that way. I didn't intend on staying so long."

"I told you, stay as long as you like. Just keep in mind there's probably a bunch of things you don't know I don't know. But I enjoy having you around just the same."

She smiled. Rick liked having her to take care of. She didn't mind terribly *being* taken care of, but also knew that no matter how he felt about it, this was a temporary arrangement at best.

The road exit led to a large main street, and then—following a lengthy series of talking map commands—along side roads and into what appeared to be a residential neighborhood.

"You're sure about this?" Rick asked. "This is pretty *Leave it to Beaver* out here."

"I don't know what that means."

"I mean this doesn't look like a… oh, hey, never mind I guess."

The termination of the directions was at a house on the corner of two streets. The lawn extended to the sidewalk, and there was a sign embedded in the lawn, which bore the doctor's legend next to an artfully rendered caduceus.

"There's your doctor's office," Rick said. "Guess I shouldn't have expect something that looked like a hospital."

~

The entrance to the medical office was through a side door leading to what might otherwise have been a basement apartment. They were greeted there by a tall, thin, older (human) man with a warm smile and a cold handshake. He introduced himself as Dr. Marks and led them to his reception area—a small space with a plywood floor beneath a dozen padded metal chairs, plus another three around a short desk. The walls were lined with empty bookshelves and the space had a faint scent of mildew.

"Now, which of you is the patient!" the doctor asked with a kind of manufactured enthusiasm. "I'm afraid the notes I have on this appointment aren't at all clear."

"There's a complicated answer to that," Rick said.

"Ah, well, in this world of ours there are a lot of complicated things, aren't there?" He winked. "Please, sit!"

Marks stepped behind his desk and sat in a weathered office chair as she and Rick took less comfortable metal chairs on the other side of the desk. Having never been to a medical doctor for professional reasons, Eve was uncertain how much of the inherent unwelcoming sense of this room was a product of this particular doctor, and how much was standard for all such offices. Either way, aside from their host's rehearsed jocularity, she didn't feel welcome.

The doctor slipped on a pair of glasses and took a closer look at both of them. "If I could be a tiny bit forward, here… Rick is it? And you're Eve. I am *terrible* with names, so you'll have to excuse me if I say them five or ten times over. But I'm going to go out on a limb and say *neither* of you is here for me. Professionally, I mean."

"That's so, yes," Eve said.

"Why do you say that, doctor Marks?" Rick asked. "I mean, it's true, but what gave it away?"

He smiled. "Son, if someone handed you one of my business cards, you already know why. I don't treat humans down here. A few times a month I work a rotation down at Saint Jude's and then I'll see humans, but out here I serve another kind of client. *You* are definitely human. Her, I'm not completely certain."

"I am," she said.

"You need some *sun!*" he said with a laugh. "Someone might come after you with a stake one day."

"My eyes are the wrong color and it's still daytime, but I understand your point."

"Yes of course, *I* know your eyes are the wrong color, but someone else might not. Thank goodness for those silly movies, people nowadays think much more highly of vampires—"

"Hold up," Rick interrupted. "No, you know what? Never mind. I'm all the way on the other side of the looking glass already here."

"Now, were you testing me, Rick? Was this why you came?"

"Nah, I just wanted to hear someone else say this stuff. I've been getting it from her for a few weeks now, and I figured either I was losing my mind or she'd already lost hers."

"You look healthy to me," he said to Eve, in a way that sounded like a compliment and not a lascivious assertion. This was perhaps a talent a medical doctor would have to develop, given how often he had to ask people to remove clothing for clinical reasons.

"So, now that we all agree the world is full of stranger things than us, what can I help you with?"

"I have a number of questions," Eve said. "But we actually *have* brought you a patient."

"Oh! Are they still in the car? You can bring them in, certainly."

"No, they're here. Dee, would you say hello to the doctor?"

Dee hovered in front of his face.

"H'lo," she said.

Dr. Marks nearly fainted.

~

"I'd heard of them, of course, but I never expected to *meet* one!" Dr. Marks said, a little later. He was looking at Dee under a magnifying glass, and Dee, to her credit, was sitting still for him. It helped that Rick had mushrooms in his pocket for her once this was over.

They had moved to the doctor's examination room, which

was a brightly lit and far more impressively antiseptic area behind a cheap wooden door near the desk in his waiting room. This had more of the feel Eve was expecting on a visit to a medical practitioner: stocked shelves full of sealed containers of clean objects, all the surfaces silvery and gleaming, and the ever-present aroma of rubbing alcohol.

"And they're self-aware, you say?" he asked. "And intelligent?"

"Of course," Eve said. "You conversed with her."

"So I did. Hello, little pixie, aren't you remarkable!"

"H'lo," Dee said.

He put the glass away.

"The condition you described the other one in, have you seen anything like that in this... Dee is it?"

"No, but we saw Cee in an advanced stage of deterioration. I couldn't say how it began, or what that beginning looked like. But you've never treated a pixie before, so I imagine you wouldn't know what to look for either."

"I'm afraid I haven't. Intelligent or not, if she has no way to way to pay for treatment, I'm afraid it wouldn't be customary for me to offer care. A veterinarian, possibly."

"You think the pet shop has a pixie doc?" Rick asked.

"Probably not. I also don't think it would occur to one to seek medical help."

"She looks healthy to you, though?" Eve asked.

"Sure. But as you've pointed out, I don't know what to look for, so I'm not sure how much help I can really offer."

Eve considered asking if he had ever witnessed a dead demon, but decided against doing so. It seemed unlikely that the man who lived in this large house and nice suburban neighborhood would be familiar with the likes of a demon. A battlefield surgeon might have more applicable experience.

"The elf who gave me your card, he was sick. He'd been to see you recently."

"I see lots of elves, sure. I'd ask you to give me a name to narrow it down, but we're going to hit a real problem with patient confidentiality. I really can't talk about anyone's sickness without them here to provide consent. You understand."

"I do."

She had never even asked the elf for his name. The idea that he might be difficult to re-locate or that he may not be sufficiently unique and therefore require a title was one that hadn't occurred.

"This was… it would have been over two weeks since you saw him. You provided pills for his condition. I'm not asking for details on his disease specifically, but if there was another being in your office displaying symptoms for a similar disease as that which killed Cee… I'm asking if you see any evidence of that in Dee."

"Like I said, she looks healthy, for whatever that's worth."

It was such a simple question: did the elf have the same disease as that which she described? The doctor seemed constitutionally incapable of responding to direct questions because of his odd confidentiality rules to protect a patient whose identity she couldn't even provide.

Rick gave it a try. "Doctor, what we're basically wondering is if you've ever seen or heard of a condition like the one we're talking about. Whether you saw it in this one patient or in any patient of yours ever."

"Well no, I haven't, but I can ask around and see if anyone else has. This probably doesn't come as a surprise but the kind of doctor that specializes in these sorts of clients… we all know one another. I'm pretty sure I'd remember seeing one of mine melting, so fair to say I never have, but maybe someone else has. Do you have any reason to think what would do that to a pixie would do the same thing to an adult of any other kind of species?"

"That can happen, right? A virus can jump from one species to another. Happens all the time."

"Yes, yes, Rick, you aren't wrong. What I mean is it's unusual for us to see the same impact. It's less common for the same thing to cause fatalities in small things *and* in big things. Like… this is a silly example, but caffeine is poisonous to certain bugs, but humans can't get enough of it. Or better, a dose of rat poison sufficient to kill a rat is not generally adequate to kill a person. It's a question of scale. There's a version of the ebola virus fatal to monkeys but manifests as a head cold in people. It can go the other direction as well. Malaria doesn't kill mosquitos, but it will do a lot to a human. Now, something interesting enough to do what you've described to a pixie and also to an elf, I see no reason it wouldn't do the same to both of *you*, yet neither of you appear to be sick. I have no reason to think such a thing would be possible."

They're all the same. Don't you see? Dream-Adam said yet again.

The dream ran counter to the doctor's experience, though, and since Dr. Marks was real and the Adam in her head was not, she felt intellectually obligated to believe the medical man. Emotionally, though, the figment of her nightmare was the one she sided with.

"Where'd the pills come from?" Rick asked.

"I'm sorry?"

"She said the elf had some pills to help him get better. Do you doctors have your own pharmacy too?"

"Ah, now *that* I can talk about! Rick, there are a number of medical conditions specific to one species or another, and many of them require a unique treatment. Often that treatment is common and mundane. For instance, imps are horribly allergic to pistachios, but the cure is a shot of drambuie. But there are some conditions requiring more… exotic things, and some of those things don't exist in a natural form anywhere, or they do but in such small amounts as to be effectively non-existent as a cure for a large sub-culture.

"Understand that those of us in this field, much of the time we're working with… shall we say, *traditional* cures. Holistic, even. You could argue a professional such as myself is as much a historian as a medical man. This is why we all keep in touch, you see. There are no laboratories working on cures for these folks. There aren't enough of them to treat, and established medical science doesn't know they exist anyway."

"Yet you have pills," Eve said.

"Yes. There are several manufacturing facilities that, in addition to producing supplements for human consumption, provide us with pills for various ailments. Now, let me say… hopefully I can phrase this in a reasonable way… It's *possible* I know the elf you spoke to. I do recall one a few weeks back with what I'd call flu-like symptoms. Nothing too terribly serious, and to be honest it was probably a bug he picked up from a human. That happens quite a lot with goblins and elves, as they're very close to us and some flu viruses are sufficiently indiscriminate. Viruses work much the same in elves as in humans as well. Once they have it, it's mostly about getting them comfortable and allowing their own immune systems to rally. But for elves, there's a tree root extract that does a marvelous job of boosting their natural immunity. The problem is, the root is from a baobab tree, which is native to only a few places on Earth, and we aren't in one of those places. An extract is available in pill form, however. Here."

He opened one of the drawers built into his wall, and pulled out a white plastic bottle. He tossed it to Rick.

"These are made by a local company, actually. They're only about thirty miles from here. Good people."

Rick took a look at the label, then opened the bottle.

"They smell," he noted.

"Sure do. Have one! They won't do a thing for you, but they won't hurt you either."

"No thanks."

Rick moved to hand the bottle back, but Marks waved him off. "It's all right, we broke the seal. May as well hang onto it."

"Right."

"The elf I met... I touched his skin and it felt... sticky. Gummy, almost. Can you... did you observe anything like this?"

"Not that I recall, Eve. Was it a hot day?"

"Yes, it was."

"If he still had the flu, he was probably fighting a fever. Elves can get really clammy. It was probably something as simple as that. You're lucky you didn't pick up anything if you were that close to him, to be honest. Someone with his symptoms I'd be recommending bed rest to. If he was out, there's a good chance he was infecting the people around him."

"Thank you, yes. I'm sure I was lucky."

She saw no need to discuss her own immune system with the doctor. That would lead to a much longer conversation.

"And again, I don't see how a pixie and an elf could get hit with the same thing like that. If it can jump between those two species, there's no reason to think it wouldn't also jump to humans. I appreciate your concern, but I don't think you need to worry about Dee, or any other friends you might have concerns over. Keep my card, of course! I love references! And like I said I can ask around. If you kids want to leave contact information, I'll be happy to phone you up if something shakes out."

"That'd be great, sure," Rick said. He pulled out a business card of his own and put it on the desk. The doctor slid it into she pocket of his shirt, and stood.

"If there's nothing else?"

"No, thank you," Eve said. "I thought... it's something I made up, I suppose. I thought it was possible they were all the same in some way."

"All *they* who?"

"Non-human beings. Something that could connect them to one another, perhaps medically. It was a notion. But I imagine if there were, you would know."

"I know what you're saying, sure. But as far as I'm aware, the only thing connecting them is that none of my neighbors are aware they exist. Biologically, they're as different as birds and dogs."

~

By the time they reached the car, Eve had talked herself into the idea that the doctor was probably right: she was making something out of nothing. An awful thing had happened to Cee; that was undeniable. But if Dee looked healthy and felt okay and the elf she spoke to just had a flu—and was receiving medical care for it—there was nothing else to worry about.

It was interesting, then, that as soon Rick pulled away from the curb he was ready with an opinion that differed significantly.

"That was some bullshit," he said.

She laughed. "Now *your* gut is bothering you?"

"It sure is. I'm not a hundred percent sure that man's even a doctor."

"He has a sign with the staff of Hermes, that's usually a positive indication."

"Sure, and he rotates at the hospital, fine, maybe he's a *human* doctor, but I'm not buying anything he had to say about the other kind."

My paranoia may be the only infectious thing here, she thought.

"Tell me why you say this."

"Well all right, I'm not any kind of doctor, right? But I know what science is supposed to sound like, and it's not extract of some exotic tree root and a shot of drambuie. I mean, look at this."

He dropped the pill bottle into her hands.

"You want to tell me these people… these whatever-you-want-to-call-them… tell me they're real? Okay. Goblins, elves, something called an imp, why not? They're real. We'll roll with it and keep on going. But now tell me the only choice they have for medical care is witch-doctor pills from that guy, and I'm sorry, something's gone wrong."

"I'm unfamiliar with how medicine is made, but I know a number of herbal remedies. This doesn't seem unreasonable to me."

"Sure, but these things get tested, okay? Look, I get a headache, I can either take an herbal supplement or I can take some medicine. I *have* that option, because at some point someone took the time to do some scientific testing on some things and came up with a drug that will help me with my headache, and if I don't like the idea of taking a drug I can take some gingko extract or rub some tea leaves on my eyelids or whatever. But from what I just heard, if I'm an elf and I'm not feeling well, I have to go see doctor here-try-this, handing out tree roots and calling it drugs."

She took a look at the label on the bottle. The company name was Holitix, which meant nothing to her. The bottle had a symbol on it that did look familiar, but she wasn't sure if she could place it correctly, historically.

"This is very old," she said.

"The remedy?"

"The markings in their house symbol. Beside their name."

He laughed. "The company logo."

"Yes."

"Let me see?"

He was pulling back onto the highway. It always unnerved her when she was being driven by someone who was also speaking, or otherwise not devoting full attention to the road. She didn't know how to drive and didn't expect she would ever put herself in a position to learn, so it was possible she was overreacting. Perhaps it was easy. It seemed more probable that the apparent ease gave the driver a false comfort and allowed them to ignore how often they were flirting with a horrible death.

"Please just watch the road. I'll describe it. It's an X, with a line connecting the top of the left-and-right diagonal so the X looks like a sort of table. On top of the horizontal line are three vertical marks that are fatter in the bottom half than in the top half. They look like bottles, nearly."

"Huh. Doesn't sound like anything I've seen before. Probably just an artistic design. Medicines on a table."

"That may well be what it *means*, but where it comes from… It's very, very old."

"How old? Older than you?"

"No. The Earth is older than me. Few other things are. Perhaps we can use your computer to figure out where it comes from."

"Do you think it's important?"

"I don't know. But doctor Marks said when he needs exotic remedies he goes to this company, and you've said there should be real science behind the remedies. If we want to satisfy your concerns, we will need to learn more about Holitix."

"*My* concerns? This was all your idea."

"It was. It may still be. My instinct is to assume the worst about this world, Rick. I'd like to believe this time I am wrong, and the reasoning he provided was sound."

"An hour ago I would have been there with you. I'm not so sure now."

"Yes. But you also just learned there were other sentient creatures living in your shadows. I would say this makes you temporarily predisposed to conspiratorial thinking."

He laughed. "I'm gonna call in sick to work this week and tell them that's what I got. I bet they'll be cool with it."

~

The markings in the Holitix logo were in a script called Vinca, a meaningless title given by whichever modern archeologist was responsible for assigning the ancient alphabet a name. *Vinca*—the word—had no correlation to the root name or communal origin of the people who used the alphabet, but Eve also couldn't remember what they called themselves, so Vinca it was.

The meaning she understood well enough. Vinca wasn't a language in the modern sense: the symbols didn't represent sounds in a spoken tongue. This was a pictographic language, and so in this instance the symbol meant exactly what it looked like: bottles on a table. It was a representation of a shop or, in this instance, an apothecary.

It made for an interesting choice in company design, but Eve wasn't sure it was anything more than that.

Rick's research into the company, meanwhile, had taken on an even more conspiratorial bent. He looked into Holitix's finances —legally, she assumed—and discovered a parent company that sold vitamins, breakfast cereal, and a few other things. He ascribed great significance to this, but when she tried to grasp why, she fell short.

His next steps were to map out the reach—market and geographic—of the entire conglomerate, believing it proved something Eve also couldn't see or fully understand.

"Imagine if each of these factories is putting out stuff like this…" he held the pill bottle aloft, "…from the back door at the same time the stuff they advertise is going out the front."

"That appears to be their business approach, I agree," Eve said. "I'm trying to understand what it is you find troubling. The populations they are servicing are powerfully secretive, this seems only appropriate."

"Sure, sure," he said. And then he fell silent.

This happened a lot over the next few weeks. Rick acted like he was struggling with an idea he couldn't put voice to, and these daily forays into the Holitix company architecture was the only way he could wrestle effectively with the concept.

Eve was ready to put the whole thing behind her and move on, which possibly meant leaving the relative comfort of Rick's home and developing a more thoroughly independent existence in the world. She'd been with him long enough to recognize that what had at first been a moment of convenience—specifically, a sexual need and a willing partner—had become a longer-term arrangement, and it was an arrangement that wasn't going to allow her to accomplish what she wished. It was easy enough to be taken care of, but it wasn't precisely a novelty, and she hated thinking of herself as dependent.

It was possible *this* was what Rick actually struggled over, whether consciously or not. So long as the death of Cee was *their* problem, she wouldn't leave. His need to solve the Holitix mystery might have been rooted in an interest in keeping Eve around.

While Rick toiled with uncovering a conspiracy he seemed the only one to recognize, Eve tried to solve the matter the only way *she* could: by finding the sick elf again and confirming his good health. If she could verify the efficacy of the pills and the doctor's care, it may go far in assuaging their worries and convincing Rick to relax.

The problem was, she couldn't find the elf. Each day, as before, she returned to the marketplace to reconnect with him, and each day she failed to do so.

It didn't mean anything, of course. It was a busy part of the city, and there was no reason to assume he traveled through the market as a matter of habit. Or he quit, or lost his job, or any number of a hundred other explanations. All that *could* be drawn from it was that the elf was not going to be the solution she'd hoped for him to be.

Unless… he *hadn't* gotten better. Unless he was dead, and she had been right all along.

She decided not to tell Rick, and to believe that *not* finding the elf didn't mean what it could have meant. But each day that went by without him turning up made the benign explanation harder to accept.

~

"Here's what bothers me," Rick said one night.

They were out on his porch at the time, enjoying the cool evening breeze and sated appetites, having dined and made love. Both experiences were very pleasant, if less than ardent. Dee was buzzing around, which was something they had gotten so used to they sometimes forgot it was an unusual thing.

"Did you know the government used to conduct experiments on handicapped kids?"

"No. Which government?"

"This one. The U.S. government."

"I didn't know that, no."

Eve was aware of thousands of atrocities committed by hundreds of governments. She couldn't imagine this particular atrocity was any worse than the others. Such was the nature of this world.

"The reason, right, is that a handicapped kid is still a human kid, so if you're gonna test a medication or see how people respond to a certain kind of radiation, or if you want to figure out how many doses of a poison it takes to kill somebody, why *not* try it out on someone who's already a throwaway person, right? By the standards of the time, I mean. Same thing happened to black people in the Fifties in a couple of places. Biologically human, but also not considered human. Do you get what I'm saying?"

"Perhaps. You're wondering what would happen if someone decided to conduct experiments on certain non-humans."

"I'm wondering if they already *are* conducting those experiments. The pills from Holitix… we don't know what's in them, and they're going to market in a shadow industry to patients nobody is supposed to know even exist. And it's not like they're making money off of the pills. Marks had a drawer full of these and he just handed over one bottle like it was nothing. Lemme ask you: if one of these folks die, what happens?"

"It's handled quietly. Internally, within the community."

"So, if a human businessman melts in his own apartment, we're gonna see it in the news. But if it's an elf?"

"I see what you mean now."

"There's no accountability here! The FDA isn't going to be checking on these pills, and neither is anyone else. So what if? What if those tree root pills aren't just doing nothing, what if it's worse than that? What if they're doing *something* and it's a bad something."

"You're forgetting Cee. She wasn't taking the pills, and we don't know how she even got sick."

"Yeah. Yeah, I know. And there's no business incentive that makes any sense here. If the company has a market cornered on a specific kind of customer, poisoning that customer is poor financial planning, whether it's accidental or not. Plus, as the doctor said, they're as different as birds and dogs. The money would be in running under-the-radar experiments on non-humans to test drugs meant *for* humans."

"Yes. All of that is true, provided money is the goal."

"Not that you're wrong, but what other goal would a corporation have?"

"I don't know. But motives can be complex and not necessarily guided by reason. Presumptions to the contrary have brought down kingdoms."

~

A week after that conversation, just prior to dinner, Rick received a phone call from Dr. Marks.

"I wanted to let you both know I asked around, and it looks like I may owe you an apology," he said. Eve could hear him clearly because, on receiving the call, Rick hit a button to make the cellular phone loud enough for them to both hear. *On speaker* was what he called it. This was another of the things Eve still had to make time to adjust to.

"I don't think you need to apologize for anything," Rick said. "But what's up?"

"As it turns out, there does appear to be something new going around. I described the symptoms to a few colleagues, and surprisingly, they *have* seen it. And not in pixies, either. Incidentally, they were *very* jealous that I got to see one."

"So, there may be something happening," Eve said, loudly, directly at the phone. Rick made a signal with his hand to suggest she lower her voice. *Talk normal*, he mouthed.

"May be, yes. Hello, Eve. That brings me to the other reason I called. We're having a symposium of sorts. It's not at all formal, since there are only six of us, but we like to meet every couple of months, and it's really useful when something like this turns up. Our next meeting is in a couple of days, and I thought it would be wonderful if the two of you could stop by and talk about what you observed. We need to, *level-set*, let's say, and I think it would help. Figure out what we can figure out and all that."

"Two days?" Rick repeated. "Yeah, I think we can do that. Where do we go?"

Marks read out the address. It was familiar to both of them.

"Isn't that the Holitix building?" Rick asked.

"It's one of them! We all do a little consulting for Holitix. These meetings are as much feedback for their benefit as for ours. I'll introduce you, they're great people."

Rick shot her a look she couldn't entirely read. He was either wary or excited.

"That sounds great," he said.

"So you'll be there?"

"Absolutely, count us in."

"I'm so glad! And don't worry about dinner, we cater the whole thing. Oh! And before I forget, would it be possible to bring your pixie friend? As I said, everyone's jealous. We promise, nothing invasive."

SIX

The Holitix factory was on what Rick called an *industrial road*, and it wasn't difficult to understand why. Every building on the road was a corporate structure of some sort, each announced with large stone-and-metal signs at the base of long drives leading away from the road. It reminded Eve of war battlements: fortresses of soldiers established far from population centers, ready to strike out on long campaigns with a word from the emperor.

The building itself was less fortress-like. The designers didn't appear concerned with siege engines or defensive measures against heavy infantry. There was also none of the security measures she expected, like tall fences or a gated lot. She and Rick simply left the road, drove up the hill and around a corner, and arrived in their parking area.

It was toward the end of the business day, so most of the workers were at the same time driving down the hill and away from the office park, which made finding a spot for the car that was near the entrance simple enough.

"Doesn't look all that ominous," Rick said, as they climbed out.

"You were expecting something else?"

"Maybe, yeah. More mad-scientist-y."

She wasn't sure what that meant. A movie reference, possibly.

"You were concerned. I know you joke, but you were concerned."

He squinted at the building—the setting sun was lighting up the windows—rather than looking at her. It was a behavior she learned to expect when he spoke of serious matters. He preferred to address a non-specific area in the distance instead of the person he was addressing. It was a curious quirk.

"I was, and I guess I am still. I mean, *here*, this is where this meeting is happening, right? It feels dumb to think like this because we're, you know, in the real world, but I'd have been a whole lot more relaxed if Dr. Marks had given us just about any other address. Like, if this weren't me and I was watching me do this I'd be screaming, 'it's a trap, Rick, don't go in there!'"

"We don't have to go in, we can just leave."

"Can't do that, because I'm an adult. It's like when you're alone in the dark and you talk yourself into there being something in the room with you, but then you remember you're not a kid, and you don't get to be afraid of the dark any more."

"Sometimes the dark does hide things. It's a good instinct."

"Yeah, remind me not to share childhood stories with you."

She grabbed his hand and squeezed it.

"We don't have to go in only to satisfy my curiosity, but if we do and you're concerned, I can protect you."

He laughed, and kissed her on the forehead. "Thanks, that's sweet. Let's just go in, I feel stupid worrying about a super-villain lair while overweight white guys are driving past me in Hondas."

Dee buzzed past his head.

"Yeah, you too, c'mon."

A glass entryway led to a reception desk manned by a portly man with a cloth version of a badge sewn into his shirt. Rick approached the desk to introduce them, but only got as far as his name before he was interrupted.

"Yes, we were told to expect you," he said, with the perfunctory smile of a man whose job didn't depend on his courtesy seeming genuine. He placed two plastic VISITOR badges on the counter. "Have a seat, someone will be down to fetch you in a minute."

He pointed them to a lounge area defined only by furniture that, when used, turned out to be much too firm to be truly comfortable.

"It's like I'm here for a job interview," Rick said with a smile. "Weird how these places make a person feel as if they don't belong."

"I feel like that nearly everywhere," she said. "Is this protocol normal?"

"For a secure building? Sure. I think it'd be weird if we were just told to head on up somewhere."

They waited on the couch for a time, as employees, dressed in variations of the business-casual she'd seen so often in the marketplace, passed by on the way to their cars.

Presently, a woman in a skirt suit with thick legs and spiky short hair approached. Like the security guard and everyone else who'd walked past, she appeared to be a human.

"Hi, I'm Margaret? I'm here to take you down."

Everyone shook hands.

"We were expecting Dr. Marks," Rick said.

She nodded and gave a smile only slightly warmer than the one the man at the desk had for them. It was broad, but never reached her eyes. Eve decided she didn't like her.

"I'm only supposed to bring you down," Margaret said, "but I expect he's already here. The meeting's about to start."

Rick glanced at Eve. He looked modestly uncomfortable about this arrangement and appeared to be looking for permission to proceed. She felt similarly discomfited, but was still more curious than concerned. She gave him a tiny nod.

"Sure, of course," he said to their host. "Lead on."

Dee buzzed along as they walked, either unnoticed or ignored by everyone else: surprising only in that Marks had invited her as well. Rick opened his shirt pocket and made a silent waving gesture he'd trained the pixie to recognize. She flew into the pocket and settled in. He closed his light jacket to disguise the tiny bulge she made.

Rick shrugged, as if to say *I don't know how this happened but I own a pixie now*. Eve nearly laughed.

Margaret brought them to a bank of elevators, choosing a specific one that required she wave a plastic card over a panel with a red light before the door would open. Eve noted with some curiosity that the other elevators didn't have any kind of panel. It was perhaps unsurprising, then, that their elevator went down instead of up.

"Whoa," Rick said. "Didn't expect that."

"Yes, the sub-levels can be a shock," Margaret said. "It's where we do the things that aren't in the company brochures. Most people here never get a chance to see this part of the facility."

"What sort of things?" Eve asked.

"Oh well… I shouldn't say. I assumed… never mind, don't mind me. I'm just supposed to bring you to the room."

"Sounds ominous," Rick said.

"Wasn't supposed to, sorry. It's an ordinary old conference room."

"Not the room part, the other part."

"I didn't mean to imply anything terrible. It's the clientele that's the secret, if you understand my meaning."

The elevator stopped and dinged, announcing their arrival at sub-level C, and the doors slid open.

Ahead of them was a long corridor, well lit and not particularly unpleasant-looking save for the part where it was underground and starved of any natural lighting.

It reminded Eve of a crypt: a very bright crypt, but a crypt nonetheless.

Rick seemed to be sharing in her unease.

"Tell me again where we're going?" he asked.

"Oh, just down to the end of the hall. Come on."

Margaret led them out of the elevator. They followed, reluctantly, and perhaps only because no other options were presented.

"I know," Margaret said as they walked, "the first time I came down here I was a little creeped out. We tried to brighten it up, but I think there's only so much you can do. We put some plants in the hall a couple of times, but they kept dying and that just made it worse. It's like the body can sense when it's below the ground. It's always chilly too. Do you feel it?"

"I do," Eve said. "It's unpleasant."

"I know. But, you know, you get used to it."

"Tell me, do a lot of people work down here?"

"Not a lot, no," Margaret said. "There are more labs than scientists, I'll be honest. But we're still building out."

The corridor was bringing them past glass doors which themselves led to other internal corridors. At each door was a set of pegs from which hung identical white cloth coats. They were laboratories, Eve decided, and these were protective garments.

It called into question Rick's concern that no real science was being performed in this facility. Eve didn't know exactly what *real* science was versus any other kind, but active laboratories seemed like a strong positive indicator. Although she didn't know what they were working on, and couldn't be certain that the same set-up would or wouldn't be required in a place where holistic vitamins were manufactured.

Ahead, the corridor ended at a set of steel doors with rubberized seals on their borders. The doors were the full height of the corridor.

"What's in there?" Rick asked. "Is that where we're going?"

"No, no," Margaret said. "That's a storage room. We're over here, last room on the left."

There were wooden double-doors to the left and the right. They were neither see-through glass like the ones behind nor steel like the ones in front. It was very much the sort of entrance one might expect of a conference room.

When Rick saw Margaret pull out keys to unlock the door, he made the obvious observation.

"So I guess they aren't here ahead of us."

"Who's that?"

"The doctors we're here to meet. Because you're unlocking that door there, so…"

"Well you might be the first ones here after all!" She turned from Rick. "So, you're *Eve*, right?"

It was a confusing question.

"I am."

"I mean, *the* Eve. We've heard a lot about you, that's all."

And then all the lights in the corridor went out.

Hands grabbed Eve from behind—how did she not notice someone behind her?—and she was lifted and pushed forward so fast she lost her footing and fell awkwardly onto a rough carpet.

She heard Rick call out in alarm, and then a muffled thump, and then nothing.

A door lock was engaged.

The lights came back.

She was on her knees in a conference room. A large wood table rested in the center, surrounded by leather chairs. Glass rectangles were hung along the walls, one every few feet. Televisions, she assumed.

Only one or two things can sneak up on me, she thought. *There are non-humans in this building.*

She got to her feet. The doors she'd been shoved through—the conference room doors Margaret had opened—were now closed, and a quick check verified they were indeed locked again.

None of what had just happened made sense. This was hardly a prison cell, but it could also not be called a meeting if she was alone. The darkness, the sudden violence, the separation of her from Rick… none of it was necessary to corral two parties who had arrived willingly.

The only thing self-evident was that there would be no gathering of specialist doctors for a conversation about emerging diseases in the non-human community. Beyond this, she was at a loss.

She wondered if they had hurt Rick.

I promised to protect him.

There was no sense of urgency to the thought. He was either already dead or they were keeping him alive. If it was the former, it didn't matter how quickly she acted. If it was the latter, it made sense to learn their intentions before any redress.

Whoever *they* were. That was very much an open question.

One of the television screens blinked to life. It was a still image, a picture of another picture of a fresco, depicting the goddess Demeter.

A second screen lit: Isis in a hieroglyph. Other screens: a modern artistic rendition of Hel, a statuette depicting Shiva, and on it went. Each television had a different goddess from a different culture from one historical epoch or another.

They were all female gods, and they were all Eve.

More accurately, many of the people who believed in these gods had also thought Eve was their god incarnate. Eve held the opinion that, had she not existed, the faithful's belief in their gods would have been largely unchanged.

"We know who you are."

It was a man's voice, but the owner wasn't in the room. There was a phone in the center of the conference table, but no lights were showing on it, so it wasn't coming from there either. The voice came from another source.

She chose not to respond. It didn't seem a good strategy to either confirm or disconfirm their identification, and she had nothing to ask of a man who was unwilling to show his face.

"*Why are you here?*" was the next question. It came after a lengthy pause in which she circled the table slowly, trying to get a better feel for the space.

There were air vents near the ceiling that were large enough for a pixie.

She thought she *might* know the voice.

It was incredibly difficult to be certain. There had been so many voices in her life, most of which had been quieted by death centuries ago. It didn't seem possible for there to be a man alive *now* for whom it could be said that she knew the timbre of his voice but not the owner. Worse, electronic transmission of voices altered them, sometimes to an extreme, so there was every reason to think her ears were being deceived.

But still: she thought she might know the voice.

The large screen at the back of the room blinked to life. It didn't have an image of an artist's attempt to capture the visage of a goddess. It showed another room in the building.

The camera revealed a high ceiling with lights dangling from steel latticework: a warehouse, or an unfinished area. Panning down to ground level, the room was clearly very large.

Rick had been seated in a chair in the center of the room. He looked out of breath, and someone had recently struck him in the face.

Two goblins stood at guard beside him. They were in black battle gear and armed with swords, as was their usual weapon of choice.

Eve thought their presence was as much for effect as anything, there only to assert that no matter how fast she moved, the opposition had someone faster and deadlier. It was only conditionally accurate.

Rick was probably not far.

There were other people in the room with them. She only saw Rick and the goblins, but there were shadows cast from behind the camera: lots of movement.

How many?

"*Do you care about this man?*" the voice asked. She decided it was coming from a speaker in the ceiling. To respond she had to talk skyward, as penitents might address their gods.

"I do," she said. "I would prefer you not harm him."

"*Then tell us why you are here.*"

"Tell me who I'm speaking to first. Who are you that thinks you know so much about me?"

There was no immediate response. But after the delay, one of the goblins pulled out his sword and held it to Rick's neck.

"*Tell us why you are here,*" the voice repeated.

"I'm here because I am curious. And you're a fool."

A pause. The sword was lowered.

"*Tell us why we are fools.*"

"You're a fool because you've told me already you know who I am, and because of this you should know better than to threaten one for whom I've declared affection. Look around the room, nameless man, at the exhibits you've displayed in my honor, and then understand that you should be terrified right now. I am the goddess of the hunt and the underworld and destruction and death."

The man on the other end of the speaker laughed, and then she was certain she knew him from somewhere. One can mask a speaking voice, but a laugh is impossible to disguise.

"*The gods always were a disappointment in person. We have been watching. We have seen the goddess of the hunt and death and destruction ride buses and cars, and eat, and have intercourse and sleep and shop. You* are *her. But that alone is no great thing. We know enough of you to not fear."*

She heard a buzzing. Dee had found her way into the conference room, and was flying in a circle above Eve's head.

Pixie language sounded like the wind. It was nearly impossible to speak in sentences, but words, single words, weren't difficult.

Where? was all Eve had to ask. To the man on the speaker it would have sounded like Eve performed a half-whistle, but to the pixie it was clear.

Behind wall, Dee said. She landed on the top corner of one of the flat screens to Eve's right to indicate which wall. Eve nodded.

"Once again. Tell us why you are here."

"No."

"We will kill this man, right now, while you watch. And then we will kill you. Tell us why you are here."

"Neither of those things will happen. What will happen is, he and I will walk out of this building after I have killed everyone in it."

There was silence. She waited for a goblin to raise his sword to Rick's throat again, but it didn't. She suspected whomever she was talking to had deactivated his microphone temporarily for some other reason. Perhaps he was laughing again.

"We disagree," he said, finally.

Fly home, she said to Dee. *We are safe.*

I fly home, she said back.

"Please listen carefully," Eve said to the nameless man. "I watched the birth of this world of yours. The child was violent and blood-soaked and so hungry it consumed the one that came before it. All I have witnessed since has been nothing more than an echo of that first violence. But I am *trying* to see more. I *want* to believe the beauty of a kind person's smile or a child's laugh won't eventually be washed away in a river of murder. I *want* to believe the world this one replaced is still alive inside of it somewhere.

"And so I made a vow to remain here until I found what I wanted, and I am not done looking. If you force me to break this vow, I promise by the end of the night you will know what the people who feared me as a god knew. I have no thirst for violence, but I am fluent in it. Your children with their swords and guns only think they are."

A pause, as he thought it over. It was his final opportunity to do so.

"*Tell us why you are here,*" he answered, unswayed, "*and what you know, and who else knows. Only then will we release you both. Your threats have no meaning to us.*"

It was an interesting response. He was more afraid of what she knew than of who she was. That would change.

"No," she said.

Then she stepped through the veil.

~

*T*he first time she ever crossed, she was not alone. She was taken through by a faery. His name was Unaah, and he was magnificent: head-and-shoulders taller than any human she'd ever seen, slender and powerful. Clad in only a loincloth, his lithe, pale white body seemed to carry sunlight the same way his coiled muscles carried the promise of force.

Unaah promised to take her away at a time in her life when it had been many thousands of years since she'd known anything like happiness, so of course she went, immediately and without regret.

The other side of the veil was strange at first, and at first she couldn't stay unless she was at his side. It was also warm, though, and soft, and the world she'd left—when she stayed close to the edge—was a gauzy illusion that couldn't do her harm.

In time, she learned how to stay in the veil on her own, and later how to step back over into the harsh world of her birth if and when she wanted. This was important, for as much as she adored Unaah's companionship most times, and valued him as a friend and for rescuing her from a life that might have ended poorly, she didn't love him.

He very much loved her, and she did love being loved, but it wasn't enough to compel her to remain. So one day she left him and returned to the regular world, some ten thousand years after having left it. She didn't stay long, and she didn't stay often, but from that point forward she followed the events on the plane of her birth more closely.

And whenever Unaah came looking for her, she returned to the veil and disappeared until he abandoned the search. To be found there is to want to be found.

~

When she stepped through the veil in the conference room, there was a moment of disorientation as she equilibrated, and then a warm familiarity rushed in, and she felt safe and distant from the ugly world she'd just departed. Her first instinct then was to run, abandon Rick and everyone else and bury herself deep in the recesses of this fuzzy reality.

This was always the danger of returning to this reality: the temptation to stay was too great, and the pain of leaving again too acute.

The conference room was still there. She had just stepped off the edge of the world, but she could still see it. It seemed smaller, but that was an illusion: Eve was larger. This was another strange consequence of the faery land.

As a creature of Earthly origin she could only think of these things in terms of distance. It was *wrong* to say that the further she traveled from the human plane, the larger she got, but that was what it *felt* like, and the best her mind could do. The fae had other words and ways of thinking about this that came closer, but while she could use those words in their tongue, she couldn't grasp their meaning in the same way *they* did. It was as conceptually alien as the faery land itself.

In addition to finding the world she left had gotten smaller, that world also began to move faster. Time and space had more of a variable relation to one another in the veil in contrast to a much more constant ratio on Earth, and so the further she went from the edge, the faster things appeared to move in the world. So long as she remained near, the time difference would be small, which was important. Too far in the veil and she would jump ahead to a point where it was no longer possible to save Rick.

Rick, she thought. *Focus on him.*

Dee said he was on the other side of the wall. It looked solid, but the idea of *solid* was now a far less strict limiting condition. She couldn't see through it—deeper in the veil and she would have been able to—but it wasn't an obstacle any longer.

She stood in front of the wall and put her hand against it. It *felt* solid, and offered resistance, but a gentle push and her hand was going into the stone.

It had the consistency of thick gruel, but went no deeper than the span from her fingertips to the end of her wrist. She took a deep breath and stepped through, and came out on the other side of a much larger space.

There were a dozen people in the room. The image on the television of two goblins holding Rick implied four persons total—including Rick and whoever was operating the camera—but this was no doubt an intentional deception: show enough to make the threat plain, but not enough to reveal the full measure of your resources. Those resources included men in combat gear with military weaponry at various points in the room, with a concentration on the metal doors the other side of which she and Rick had seen from the hallway.

They thought that if she came, it would be through the doors.

The man who spoke to Eve in the conference room made intelligent tactical choices that suggested he had more respect for his opponent than he was confessing. The men in the room had been warned to expect Eve, although clearly they had not been told *what* to expect, which was unfortunate for them.

The nameless man to wasn't in the room. She knew this, but couldn't say for certain how, aside from there being no obvious candidates. She still couldn't place the voice, but felt certain once she saw the owner, she would be able to.

Margaret appeared to be the closest thing to a person in charge. She was behind the camera, with a cellular telephone in her hand. She was using it in the same peculiar way Rick did when he was employing the speaker function. The face of the device was lit, held at a distance from Margaret's face.

Listening to the world from the other side of the veil was an odd experience at times, because everything was sped up. The words were still comprehensible, only a slight bit faster than normal conversation.

"If-you're-in-here," Margaret said loudly, and rapidly, "surrender-or-we'll-kill-him!"

Margaret been informed by telephone of Eve's departure, and now everyone was on alert. As anticipated, their first reaction was not to summarily execute Rick—without him in danger they had no bargaining power.

Rick looked terribly frightened, and supremely confused. He kept looking at Margaret as if ready to say something he couldn't entirely find words for, or perhaps he'd already attempted to negotiate and failed. Either way he appeared helpless, as Eve imagined anyone in his position would. She wanted to step out of the veil and tell him everything was going to be fine.

"I-know-you-can-hear-me," Margaret said. Her words piled onto one another.

I said all that needed saying already, Eve thought.

It only took a few long strides to step around Margaret and to a point behind the two goblins. They held flanking positions beside Rick, swords drawn, ready to remove his head at the first indication of violence. As the immediate obvious threats to his wellbeing, they would have to be the first to go.

Arbitrarily, she chose to begin with the goblin to Rick's right. He held his sword in his left arm, the blade flat across Rick's chest, his body in a crouch, alert and ready for every kind of attack save for the one that was about to kill him. Goblins had tremendous hearing and vision, but they were just as much creatures trapped on the Earthly plane as anyone. His battle acumen would do no good.

She pushed her right hand through his back and tried to remember where a goblin's heart was. Anatomically, they were very similar to humans, save for a slightly shorter ribcage. The heart should have been just left-of-center, as it would be in a man, unless her memory was incorrect.

There it is.

She could feel it pulsing through her fingertips.

A hand through living tissue felt only a little different than one through a solid wall, except in an organism there was the fluid motion of life. It was a little like interacting with an erratic water pipe.

She made a fist, and positioned the fist in the center of the heart.

With her left hand she grabbed the blade hilt.

Then she re-entered the world.

Snapping out of the veil was no less disorienting than traveling in the other direction. Everything slowed down and got louder and harsher. There was a smell to this plane, a vague combination of ozone, dirt and iron that was always there and had no apparent origin. Everything felt heavier.

He reappearance killed the goblin instantly. His heart exploded around her fist, and his left hand and arm shattered.

The blade fell loosely into her fingers, which gave her something to use to parry the second goblin's attack. His swing—understandably—was a little wild, aimed neither precisely at her nor at Rick. She swatted the attack away with the sword, while at the same time lowering her right arm to let the dead body attached to it slide to the floor.

Rick let out a startled scream. He had blood on his face now that wasn't his, from the detonated sword hand of the goblin, which happened right near his chin. None of the men with guns had responded, though, and Margaret understood just enough to stop speaking. Only the second goblin was fully engaged. That was something one could always count on from a goblin.

He jumped back into a precise defensive stance, the sword forward in his right hand while his left reached around the back for a second blade. He would be presenting a throwing knife momentarily.

Eve knew her way around a swordfight and thought it likely she could overpower the goblin without doing anything special—she might even, if given a moment's reflection, enjoy it—but Rick's safety was going to end up being a concern the longer the fight continued, especially once a couple of the men with the guns woke from their stupor.

She charged directly at the goblin, which left him with only one maneuver. It was a powerfully effective and efficient maneuver, however, one that would slice her in half on a diagonal if she were still there to cut. But the second before his blade struck home she crossed the veil again, passed through his attack until she was directly behind him, turned, and brought the sword around at his neck. She exited the veil in mid-swing, and took the head off cleanly.

Rick was still screaming, unless it was a continuation of the same scream. Things were happening very slowly for her, but clearly nobody else was experiencing this.

"Are you tied down?" she asked him. They were at most a

couple of steps apart and had only a little time before someone with a gun figured out how to operate it.

"Wh... what?"

He lifted his hands to wipe the blood from his eyes with the side of his sleeve.

"No you are not. Good. Take my hand."

He was still terrified, and she tried very hard not to be disappointed about this. He did get to his feet, though, and took the hand she was offering.

"Don't be alarmed," she said, and then carried him with her through the veil.

He started screaming again.

"Don't let go of my hand!" she shouted. Her voice sounded much louder and sharper. Sound was jangly and crisp and traveled far there.

He was panicking, and trying to wriggle free, and she couldn't do anything but hold on and wait for him to calm down. Slapping him would have meant dropping the sword first, and she liked the sword.

She supposed it was possible that this was a legitimately frightening experience for Rick. She couldn't entirely recall what her reaction was when first being carried across, but perhaps she too was frightened initially. Having him behave this way was no less convenient, though. The circumstances were too perilous for panic.

The space they had just occupied on Earth was being perforated by bullets from the semi-automatic machine gun one of the guards had begun firing. If they were merely invisible, they'd be dead.

The bullets tickled. She thought so, at least.

"Aaaahhh, Jesus what is... What's going ON?"

"They can't see you or hear you or hurt you so long as you *don't let go of me."*

"Why am I so tall? What *is* this??"

"Calm down, damn you."

He calmed a little, so she began dragging him to the far end of the room. It was slow-going, as he walked more or less like a man on stilts for the first time.

There was a dark corner where—once she let go of his hand—she imagined he would be safe. She led him there.

"The ground is *soft*," he said.

"Yes, and so are the walls and the ceiling. We can swim through the bedrock to the surface if you wish, but not yet."

"No, let's go! If we can go, let's just go!"

"I've made promises. I'm going to keep them this time. Now I'm going to let go of your hand. You will fall back to Earth when I do this. *Promise* you will make no sound. If you do, they will discover you. Do you understand what that will mean?"

"Yes, all right."

"You understand?"

"I understand."

She released him, and watched as he shrank to his normal height. His eyes widened and he appeared on the precipice of vomiting, but he kept silent. It was fortunate, as the men with the guns were firing around the room at every stray sound:

"Is she dead?"

"Where is she?"

"Check for a body."

"Oh my god, what did she do to him?"

"I'm gonna be sick."

Eve stepped behind one of them, inserted the sword in his forehead, and materialized until the light went out in his eyes. She stepped out again before the hail of gunfire riddled the already-dead man she was leaving behind, and also the man standing next to him.

They were so happy to use their guns they were prepared to use them on one another in a vain attempt to hit her. Bullets were indiscriminate, and firearms were what men who didn't really understand what it was like to kill used. This was why the goblins preferred swordplay. It was a sentiment she agreed with.

The man who shot at her was next. She didn't bother with subtlety, appearing next to his non-gun-hand side and using the sword until he stopped moving. Likewise the next two, whose arms she removed before they could get a shot off, then their heads to stop the screaming.

The last three threw down their guns and tried to get away. She put herself between them and the steel door exit, and made excellent use of the goblin sword. She didn't even need the veil.

That left Margaret.

The small woman had neither bothered to run nor to raise a weapon, unless the camera was considered one. She was slavishly devoted to documenting everything happening around her, and transmitting the information to whomever might be observing the video. Eve hoped it was a large audience. The more who feared her, the better.

"Do you speak to him?" Eve asked, walking slowly from the doors to the center of the room, over the remains of the unprepared soldiers.

Margaret was pointing the camera at Eve, not looking up from the view screen for the device and not answering direct questions.

"Margaret."

She looked up, confused, as if the television show she'd been watching had suddenly begun to address her directly.

Eve pressed the tip of the sword against the woman's throat. Blood from the blade dripped down Margaret's suit.

"In your hand," Eve said, "there is a telephone. Do you speak to him on this?"

"Yes" Margaret whispered. "Yes I… I do."

"What is his name?"

"I don't know."

Eve pressed the point forward. "I'll ask again."

"His name is Mr. Talbot. I don't know his first name."

"Talbot."

"Yes."

"Give it to me."

Margaret handed over the phone, and then Eve cut her throat.

She held up the phone.

"As promised, I have killed everyone," she said, over the sound of Margaret's sputtering death on the floor. "Now I'm going to find you."

A man looked at her through the glass of the telephone.

It was an impossible face. She hadn't seen it for more than a thousand years.

"I look forward to seeing you try," he said.

The screen went dark.

"Wait!" she said, but he was gone. She threw the phone across the room, and listened to it shatter on the wall. Pieces clattered to a soft ending in the blood pool of dead men.

She let the sword slide from her hand and listened to the metallic clatter as it bounced. Everything was loud and smelly and dirty again. She felt weighted down, painted in crimson and sweat.

This was the world as she'd always thought of it.

"Rick, it's time to leave," she said. Her voice was supposed to be a whisper, but it sounded so loud.

Rick didn't reply.

She checked the corner where she'd left him and found it unoccupied.

He was gone.

SEVEN

*I*t took only a little time to get from the sub-level back to the parking lot. She chose a route that didn't involve normal conveyances—stairs or elevator—and instead walked into the bedrock and pushed her way up.

It wasn't an easy trick to learn or teach. Proper technique required finding a level on the other side of the veil that was distant enough from the edge of the world to make rock as gentle as water, but with enough solidity to give one purchase. It was also very difficult to breathe in this scenario.

Still, she made the surface in what felt like only a few minutes. In Earth time it was more, which was why when she got there, Rick and his car had already driven away.

Also, the building was on fire. Loud klaxons were sounding inside and the sky was awash with red flashing lights from emergency crews approaching the road.

It was not a good time or place to step out of the veil, so she didn't.

She needed to get home to Rick, and make certain he was all right.

~

ravel in the veil was deceptively easy, although there were tricky elements if one weren't paying careful attention.

Once you understood how much smaller the world became the deeper you went, it was a simple enough thing to find a level that allowed for one stride per mile if one were so inclined. It required concentration—this was the tricky part—because time accelerated as well.

She had a way to return to Rick's home without a car, then. But if she were incautious she would advance herself a week or longer.

The pace she settled on got her back to his front door by mid-afternoon of the following day according to his clock, in about four hours of her time.

At the door, she lowered herself to the edge of the veil. Again, spacial concepts like *lowered* and *raised* and *up/down* and *far/near* were at best approximate descriptions. All it meant was her time came close to syncing with his.

She pushed through the front door and into his living room.

He was there, on the couch, drinking beer and staring at his wall. It didn't look as if he'd gotten any sleep. Dee was buzzing around, apparently ignorant of his mood.

It was good to see he had gotten home all right, and that Dee had made it as well.

I could leave him here, she thought. *He would never know.*

But there was more to talk about. He had driven away without her. She wanted to understand why, and what it meant.

She stepped out of the veil.

He seemed unsurprised when she solidified before him, but that may have been because the drink was dulling his senses.

"I was wondering if you'd come back," he said. He eyed her up and down, for long enough to make the moment uncomfortable. "That's a hell of a trick."

"It's not a trick."

"You're covered in blood. Did anyone see you like that?"

"No."

"You should shower. Probably burn those clothes or something."

Of the many things she anticipated hearing first from him, a shower wasn't on the list.

"Go ahead," he said. "I'm not going anywhere."

~

She took the shower, and changed into fresh clothing. The old clothes—it had been a pink blouse and white shorts before the events of the evening turned both to a more crimson shade—she left in a plastic bag beneath his sink. She considered following Rick's advice but had no way to make fire and didn't believe the ventilation in his living area was adequate for the smoke.

On returning to the living room, she found him essentially unmoved.

She took a chair at the table. It didn't seem the time to sit close.

"So I guess I should apologize," he said. "I figured if you came back I owed you one for not waiting."

"Where did you go?"

"There was a fire exit right there. When you dropped me out of whatever that *veil* thing was and you went over to cut people's heads off and all that... once I got past the urge to throw up I was like, I'm pretty sure everyone's too busy to even notice me, so I took off. Stairs went straight up to a side exit next to the lot, and... Honest, I'm pretty sure I didn't even think of waiting around. I just got in the car and—"

"Yes. I understand. That was the intelligent thing to do."

"I kinda freaked out."

"It's all right. I'm sorry I put you in such danger at all."

"Not sure you did. I've been running through the whole thing, right? Pretty sure it was my idea to push on this… whatever it was we stumbled over. I mean, I didn't expect anybody on the other end to be ready to kill us over a few dumb questions, not *really*. Paranoid me was all about that, but I don't think I took it that kind of serious."

"The threat was realized only after someone involved with that company recognized me for who I am. I don't imagine our lives would have been in danger otherwise. Your lone entreaties for information would have been ignored."

He nodded slowly.

"Okay. I guess that does change it a little." He pushed himself up in the couch, so their eyes were level. She could see redness on the edge of his pupils. He looked more ragged than she could remember ever seeing him.

"Recognized you for who you are, huh? So who are you?"

"You know who I am. I've told you."

"That was before you put your arm through a guy and ripped his chest open. I know who you *told* me you are, but maybe that's not right. Maybe who you told me you are is who you want to be. Who you *are* is something else."

"And what would that be?"

"I don't know. But this whole mother-of-the-world pacifism thing you have going on, I don't think I'm good with that any more."

She was trying to see this from his perspective, but it was difficult. Violence required an answer of violence. This was the dialogue of his entire world.

"I… I was protecting us," she said. "I saw no option but to answer their threat in kind."

"The guys with the swords, sure. Maybe I'll spot you both of them. Even there, though…you could have walked us both out without hurting anybody, couldn't you? Tell me I'm wrong."

"You are wrong. I *could* have, yes, I could have taken you into the veil where nobody could hurt either of us, and we could have left them bewildered and powerless to stop our exit. But that would have only sufficed for the moment. They knew your name, and I have no doubt they know where you reside. I can't keep you in the veil forever, and I can't stay here and protect you forever."

He shook his head, took a drink from his beer, and thought some more.

"Before I ran off I watched you tear apart five people. Did you leave anyone alive?

"Of course not."

"Of course not, she says. Even Margaret?"

"Yes."

"By my count that's eleven. I don't want to be worth the lives of eleven people, ever. There had to be another solution. We could've called the cops or something. Notified a congressman, or… I don't know, but we live in a civilized country where people don't just go out and kill folks with impunity. If you got me out of there I would have been okay. Did you start the fire too?"

"The… No. I saw it, but I didn't start it. I wouldn't have known how."

"Sorry, I thought maybe you can breathe fire too. I mean, why not?"

"I can't. Nobody can. Even dragons could not."

"Dragons are real, now?"

"They were. They're extinct. How did you learn of the fire?"

"It was on the news. When I saw it, first thing I thought was maybe I should call up Dr. Marks. I don't even know what I was planning to say when I reached him, but that didn't end up being a problem because his line's been disconnected. I'm kind of wondering, if I drove out there, if his place would still be standing or if it's been torched too."

"That's a real possibility, yes. Whoever was behind all of this is destroying a trail, it would be reasonable to think the doctor was one of the things that needed to be destroyed."

"He's a *person*. Not a thing to destroy."

"Don't be angry with me, I'm not the one setting the fires, I told you."

"Yeah."

He quieted, and settled on a point on the wall behind her on which to fix his gaze. She wanted to sit beside him and take his hand, and offer some sort of comfort. Something was clearly broken between them, but surely it was not permanent.

"I want you to understand," she said, once it was clear he had no new conversational thread to pull. "Violence is sometimes the only answer, but I didn't ask for it to be this way and I didn't make it this way."

"You've told me the story. But Eve, that was a… a fantasy. A myth. In this *place* where *I* live, evisceration isn't a negotiating tactic. You can talk about things that happened tens of thousands of years ago as if they're still important, but we've come a long way since. We're pretty damn civilized now."

"Are you sure?"

"Pretty sure. I can tell you the odds are good I'm the first kid on the block to witness a murder."

She laughed. "Oh, I doubt that. Whether you see it directly or not…"

"That *is* my definition of witnessing, yes."

"You enjoy the meat from the cow and then claim ignorance of her death! Your civilization no less violent than it *ever* was, only now it's committed by proxy."

It was his turn to laugh, out of surprise more than amusement.

"That's pretty good. But this is not a debate on the horrors of capitalism, wartime economies, or, I don't know, economic deprivation as a form of abuse. I can *have* that argument if you really want to, but let's keep our perspective. *You* chopped a man's head off. Let's talk about that."

"It was more than one head."

"Not helping."

"Did you not feel that your life was in danger?"

"I did, yes. And I will admit that's the first time I've been in that position. But I saw your face, Eve. When you were *doing* it, I saw your face. You can tell me all you want that you have no place here, but you didn't look unhappy. And what you were doing was something I can't imagine myself *ever* doing. I think I'd probably end up dying first."

"I didn't… No that isn't true, I didn't enjoy it. They were threatening someone I care for, and my path was clear. What you saw was the peace of clarity. I knew what I was supposed to do, and I was not going to back away from that."

Not again, she thought.

"What you were supposed to do was get us out of there safely."

"I did that."

"Without killing everybody in the building!"

"*I told him I would!*" she snapped.

When she raised her voice—something she almost never did —she saw Rick wince. It was barely a second, but it happened.

Fear.

It was then she knew she had lost him.

"Told who?" he asked.

"There was a man," she said with a forced calm. "When you and I were separated I was placed in a room where a man on a speaker claimed he knew who I was. He demanded to know what I had learned of him and his organization. I don't know why, but it seemed apparent his concern was based primarily on *my* having the information, rather than the information itself escaping. I don't know how my intervention is meant to impact whatever manner of scheme we stumbled upon."

"He didn't say?"

"Of course not. But he was convinced we knew far more than we do. Since his concern was likely keeping you alive I did not say how much or little we knew. What I did say was, if he did not let us both go, I would… do exactly what I did. I needed him to understand I wasn't bluffing, not only for that moment, but for any future moments. I gave him an opportunity to release us without any harm befalling anyone in his employ, and he chose not to listen."

"But who *is* he?"

"I don't know. I saw his face for only a moment, and thought perhaps I knew it, but I couldn't have. It isn't possible. There are only two of us, and he is not the second."

"All right. And you know there aren't others?"

"I'm as certain as I can be. Whoever he is, I have to find him, in person. I need to understand what happened last evening, and what they were doing in that laboratory. I need to learn the things he was afraid I already knew."

She looked Rick in the eye. For half a second, he met her gaze, and she thought perhaps she had been mistaken, and this situation was salvageable. Then he looked away.

"Your great conspiracy, Rick," she said. "It may be true. You can come with me. We can find out together."

He shook his head. "How?"

"I can teach you how to travel as I do. You've already seen…"

She couldn't even finish the sentence. The answer was already in his eyes. It had been since she returned.

"Look…" His voice was faltering with emotion, as he looked for more words. "I can't. I really can't."

He tried a smile, but it didn't work.

"I'm sorry. I don't… Eve, I don't want to hurt you, but…. But I don't know another way to say this. I'm a little terrified of you."

"You don't have to be. I would never hurt you."

"I appreciate that. But after what I saw… I can't *stop* seeing that. It keeps playing in my head and it won't stop. I think it's going to be there whenever I look at you. I can't make go away."

She wanted to argue, even though it would do no good.

"Yes," she said quietly. "Yes of course, I understand."

"I thought about it all night. I'm sorry."

"Yes," she smiled. She hoped it looked like a smile. "I… Well. I should *leave* you, then. I have so much… to do and you have your life to get to and…"

"I'm sorry," he repeated.

"Thank you. So am I," she said, getting to her feet.

He stood as well, and held open his arms for an embrace she was ashamed to admit she needed at all.

I am the destroyer god, she thought. *I do not need a hug.*

But she did, and he gave it to her, and she didn't want it to end.

It lasted no more than a second or two. Time on Earth may move slower than she was accustomed, but not slowly enough.

"Are you going to be okay?" he asked. He was crying a little, which seemed odd since he was the one asking her to leave. "That's the most ridiculous question I could ask, but…"

"I will be fine, Rick."

He wiped moisture from her face, and that was how she knew she was crying as well.

"Where will you go?" he asked. "To solve your mystery, I mean."

"I don't know. I have many questions and can only think of one man to ask them to. Perhaps I will."

"Who?"

"It doesn't matter…Goodbye. Take care of Dee."

She stepped into the veil.

He was going to continue talking and it was becoming less pleasant and more difficult with each word. He was full of pity and fear and she couldn't take it, and she hated him and the fact that she couldn't seem to stop weeping like a child.

The last she saw of Rick was a long, sad sigh and a return to his couch. Then she stepped through his door and down to the street and thought about all the people she'd said goodbye to in her life, and how this one, this time, hurt just a little bit more than the last ones. Perhaps it was because it was the freshest, or she'd just forgotten what it felt like.

She took a deep breath, wiped her eyes, and thought about dead pixies and elves and demons, and not Rick. Then she thought about where she would go next, and realized she wasn't at all certain.

Adam would know, she thought. If something were rotten in this world, he would know how to find it. It was one of the things he did well.

"Now I only have to figure out where you are," she said aloud, her voice echoing in the veil and heard by nobody.

Her mind made up, she put Rick behind her and began traveling deeper into the veil, to commence a search for the only immortal man on Earth.

And then, inexplicably, she sneezed.

Gene Doucette is a hybrid author, albeit in a somewhat round-about way. From 2010 through 2014, Gene published four full-length novels (*Immortal, Hellenic Immortal, Fixer,* and *Immortal at the Edge of the World*) with a small indie publisher. Then, in 2014, Gene started self-publishing novellas that were set in the same universe as the *Immortal* series, at which point he was a hybrid.

When the novellas proved more lucrative than the novels, Gene tried self-publishing a full novel, *The Spaceship Next Door,* in 2015. This went well. So well, that in 2016, Gene reacquired the rights to the earlier four novels from the publisher, and re-released them, at which point he wasn't a hybrid any longer.

Additional self-published novels followed: *Immortal and the Island of Impossible Things* (2016); *Unfiction* (2017); and *The Frequency of Aliens* (2017).

In 2018, John Joseph Adams Books (an imprint of Houghton Mifflin Harcourt) acquired the rights to *The Spaceship Next Door.* The reprint was published in September of that year, at which point Gene was once again a hybrid author.

Since then, a number of things have happened. Gene published three more novels—*Immortal From Hell* (2018), *Fixer Redux* (2019), and *Immortal: Last Call* (2020)—and wrote a new novel called *The Apocalypse Seven* that he did not self-publish; it was acquired by JJA/HMH in September of 2019. Publication date is May 25, 2021.

Gene lives in Cambridge, MA.

For the latest on Gene Doucette, follow him online

genedoucette.me
genedoucette@me.com

<u>SCI-FI</u>

The Spaceship Next Door

The world changed on a Tuesday.

When a spaceship landed in an open field in the quiet mill town of Sorrow Falls, Massachusetts, everyone realized humankind was not alone in the universe. With that realization, everyone freaked out for a little while.

Or, almost everyone. The residents of Sorrow Falls took the news pretty well. This could have been due to a certain local quality of unflappability, or it could have been that in three years, the ship did exactly nothing other than sit quietly in that field, and nobody understood the full extent of this nothing the ship was doing better than the people who lived right next door.

Sixteen-year old Annie Collins is one of the ship's closest neighbors. Once upon a time she took every last theory about the ship seriously, whether it was advanced by an adult ,or by a peer. Surely one of the theories would be proven true eventually—if not several of them—the very minute the ship decided to do something. Annie is starting to think this will never happen.

One late August morning, a little over three years since the ship landed, Edgar Somerville arrived in town. Ed's a government operative posing as a journalist, which is obvious to Annie—and pretty much everyone else he meets—almost immediately. He has a lot of questions that need answers, because he thinks everyone is wrong: the ship is doing something, and he needs Annie's help to figure out what that is.

Annie is a good choice for tour guide. She already knows everyone in town and when Ed's theory is proven correct—something is apocalyptically wrong in Sorrow Falls—she's a pretty good person to have around.

As a matter of fact, Annie Collins might be the most important person on the planet. She just doesn't know it.

～

The Frequency of Aliens

Annie Collins is back!

Becoming an overnight celebrity at age sixteen should have been a lot more fun. Yes, there were times when it was extremely cool, but when the newness of it all wore off, Annie Collins was left with a permanent security detail and the kind of constant scrutiny that makes the college experience especially awkward.

Not helping matters: she's the only kid in school with her own pet spaceship.

She would love it if things found some kind of normal, but as long as she has control of the most lethal—and only—interstellar vehicle in existence, that isn't going to happen. Worse, things appear to be going in the other direction. Instead of everyone getting used to the idea of the ship, the complaints are getting louder. Public opinion is turning, and the demands that Annie turn over the ship are becoming more frequent. It doesn't help that everyone seems to think Annie is giving them nightmares.

Nightmares aren't the only weird things going on lately. A government telescope in California has been abandoned, and nobody seems to know why.

The man called on to investigate—Edgar Somerville—has become the go-to guy whenever there's something odd going on, which has been pretty common lately. So far, nothing has panned out: no aliens or zombies or anything else that might be deemed legitimately peculiar… but now may be different, and not just because Ed can't find an easy explanation. This isn't the only telescope where people have gone missing, and the clues left behind lead back to Annie.

It all adds up to a new threat that the world may just need saving from, requiring the help of all the Sorrow Falls survivors. The question is: are they saving the world with Annie Collins, or are they saving it from her?

The Frequency of Aliens is the exciting sequel to *The Spaceship Next Door*.

Unfiction

When Oliver Naughton joins the Tenth Avenue Writers Underground, headed by literary wunderkind Wilson Knight, Oliver figures he'll finally get some of the wild imaginings out of his head and onto paper.

But when Wilson takes an intense interest in Oliver's writing and his genre stories of dragons, aliens, and spies, things get weird. Oliver's stories don't just need to be finished: they insist on it.

With the help of Minerva, Wilson's girlfriend, Oliver has to find the connection between reality, fiction, the mythical Cydonian Kingdom, and the non-mythical nightclub called M Pallas. That is, if he can survive the alien invasion, the ghosts, and the fact that he thinks he might be in love with Minerva.

Unfiction is a wild ride through the collision of science fiction, fantasy, thriller, horror and romance. It's what happens when one writer's fiction interferes with everyone's reality.

Fixer

What would you do if you could see into the future?

As a child, he dreamed of being a superhero. Most people never get to realize their childhood dreams, but Corrigan Bain has come close. He is a fixer. His job is to prevent accidents—to see the future and "fix" things before people get hurt. But the ability to see into the future, however limited, isn't always so simple. Sometimes not everyone can be saved.

"Don't let them know you can see them."

Graduate students from a local university are dying, and former lover and FBI agent Maggie Trent is the only person who believes their deaths aren't as accidental as they appear. But the truth can only be found in something from Corrigan Bain's past, and he's not interested in sharing that past, not even with Maggie.

To stop the deaths, Corrigan will have to face up to some old horrors, confront the possibility that he may be going mad, and find a way to stop a killer no one can see.

Corrigan Bain is going insane ... or is he?

Because there's something in the future that doesn't want to be seen. It isn't human. It's got a taste for mayhem. And it is very, very angry.

Fixer Redux

Someone's altering the future, and it isn't Corrigan Bain

Corrigan Bain was retired.

It wasn't something he ever thought he'd be able to do. The problem was that the *job* he wanted to retire from wasn't actually a job at all: nobody paid him to do it, and nobody else did it. With very few exceptions, nobody even knew he was doing it.

Corrigan called himself a fixer, because he fixed accidents that were about to happen. It was complicated and unrewarding, and even though doing it right meant saving someone, he didn't enjoy it. He couldn't stop —he thought—because there would always be accidents, and he would never find someone to take over as fixer. Anyone trying would have to be capable of seeing the future, like he did, and that kind of person was hard to find.

Still, he did it. He's never been happier.

His girlfriend, Maggie Trent of the FBI, has not retired. Her task force just shut down the most dangerous domestic terrorist cell in the country, and she's up for an award, and a big promotion.

Everything's going their way now, and the future looks even brighter.

Unfortunately, that future is about to blow up in their faces…literally. And somehow, Corrigan Bain, fixer, the man who can see the future, is taken completely by surprise.

Fixer Redux is the long-awaited sequel to *Fixer*. Catch up with Corrigan, as he tries to understand a future that no longer makes sense.

FANTASY

The Immortal Novel Series

Immortal

"I don't know how old I am. My earliest memory is something along the lines of fire good, ice bad, so I think I predate written history, but I don't know by how much. I like to brag that I've been there from the beginning, and while this may very well be true, I generally just say it to pick up girls."

Surviving sixty thousand years takes cunning and more than a little luck. But in the twenty-first century, Adam confronts new dangers—someone has found out what he is, a demon is after him, and he has run out of places to hide. Worst of all, he has had entirely too much to drink.

Immortal is a first person confessional penned by a man who is immortal, but not invincible. In an artful blending of sci-fi, adventure, fantasy, and humor, IMMORTAL introduces us to a world with vampires, demons and other "magical" creatures, yet a world without actual magic.

At the center of the book is Adam.

Adam is a sixty thousand year old man. (Approximately.) He doesn't age or get sick, but is otherwise entirely capable of being killed. His survival has hinged on an innate ability to adapt, his wits, and a fairly large dollop of luck. He makes for an excellent guide through history ... when he's sober.

Immortal is a contemporary fantasy for non-fantasy readers and fantasy enthusiasts alike.

Hellenic Immortal

"Very occasionally, I will pop up in the historical record. Most of the time I'm not at all easy to spot, because most of the time I'm just a guy who does a thing and then disappears again into the background behind someone-or-other who's busy doing something much more important. But there are a couple of rare occasions when I get a starring role."

An oracle has predicted the sojourner's end, which is a problem for Adam insofar as he has never encountered an oracular prediction that didn't come true ... and he is the sojourner. To survive, he's going to have to figure out what a beautiful ex-government analyst, an eco-terrorist, a rogue FBI agent, and the world's oldest religious cult all want with him, and fast.

And all he wanted when he came to Vegas was to forget about a girl. And maybe have a drink or two.

The second book in the Immortal series, Hellenic Immortal follows the continuing adventures of Adam, a sixty-thousand-year-old man with a wry sense of humor, a flair for storytelling, and a knack for staying alive. Hellenic Immortal is a clever blend of history, mythology, sci-fi, fantasy, adventure, mystery and romance. A little something, in other words, for every reader.

Immortal at the Edge of the World

"What I was currently doing with my time and money ... didn't really deserve anyone else's attention. If I was feeling romantic about it, I'd call it a quest, but all I was really doing was trying to answer a question I'd been ignoring for a thousand years."

In his very long life, Adam had encountered only one person who appeared to share his longevity: the mysterious red-haired woman. She appeared throughout history, usually from a distance, nearly always vanishing before he could speak to her.

In his last encounter, she actually did vanish—into thin air, right in front of him. The question was how did she do it? To answer, Adam will have to complete a quest he gave up on a thousand years earlier, for an object that may no longer exist.

If he can find it, he might be able to do what the red-haired woman did, and if he can do that, maybe he can find her again and ask her who she is … and why she seems to hate him.

But Adam isn't the only one who wants the red-haired woman. There are other forces at work, and after a warning from one of the few men he trusts, Adam realizes how much danger everyone is in. To save his friends and finish his quest he may be forced to bankrupt himself, call in every favor he can, and ultimately trade the one thing he'd never been able to give up before: his life.

$$\sim$$

Immortal and the island of Impossible Things

"I thought I'd miss the world."

Adam is on vacation in an island paradise, with nothing to do and plenty of time to do nothing.

It's exactly what he needed: beautiful weather, beautiful girlfriend, plenty of books to read, and alcohol to drink. Most importantly, either nobody on the island knows who he is, or, nobody cares.

"This probably sounds boring, and maybe it is. It's possible I have no compass to help determine boring, or maybe I have a different threshold than most people. From my perspective, though, the vast majority of human history has been boring, by which I mean nothing happened, and sure, that can be dull. On the other hand, nothing happening includes nobody trying to kill anybody, and specifically, nobody trying to kill me. That's the kind of boring a guy can get behind."

Nothing last forever, though, and that includes the opportunity to *do* nothing. One day, unwelcome visitors arrive in secret, with impossible knowledge of impossible events, and then the impossible things arrive: a new species.

It's *all* impossible, especially to the immortal man who thought he'd seen all there was to see in the world. Now, Adam is going to have to figure out what's happening and make things right before he and everyone he loves ends up dead in the hot sun of this island paradise.

~

Immortal From Hell

Not all of Adam's stories have happy endings

"Paris is romantic and quests are cool. But the threat of a global pandemic kind of sours the whole thing. The good news was, if all life on Earth were felled by a plague, it looked like this one could take me out too. It'd be pretty lonely otherwise."

--Adam the immortal

When Adam decides to leave the safety of the island, it's for a good reason: Eve, the only other immortal on the planet, appears to be dying, and nobody seems to understand why. But when Adam—with his extremely capable girlfriend Mirella—tries to retrace Eve's steps, he discovers a world that's a whole lot deadlier than he remembered.

Adam is supposed to be dead. He went through a lot of trouble to fake that death, but now that he's back it's clear someone remains unconvinced. That wouldn't be so terrible, except that whoever it is, they have a great deal of influence, and an abiding interest in ensuring that his death sticks this time around.

Adam and Mirella will have to figure out how to travel halfway across the world in secret, with almost no resources or friends. The good news is, Adam solved the travel problem a thousand years earlier. The bad news is, one of his oldest assumptions will turn out to be untrue.

Immortal From Hell is the darkest entry in the Immortal series.

~

Immortal: Last Call

"I'm something like sixty-thousand years old, and I've probably thought more

about my own death than any living being has thought about any subject, ever. I used to be unduly preoccupied with what might constitute a "good death", although interestingly, this has always been an after-the-fact analysis. What I mean is, following a near-death experience, I'll generally perform a quiet review of the circumstances and judge whether that death would have been objectively good, by whatever metric one uses for that kind of thing. I'm not nearly that self-reflective while in the midst of said near-death experience. Facing death, the predominant thought is always not like this."

A disease threatening the lives of everyone—human and non-human—has been loosed upon the world, by an arch-enemy Adam didn't even know he had.

That's just the first of his problems. Adam's also in jail, facing multiple counts of murder, at least a few of which are accurate. He may never see the inside of a courtroom, because there remains a bounty on his head—put there by the aforementioned arch-enemy—that someone is bound to try to collect while he's stuck behind bars.

Meanwhile, Adam's sitting on some tantalizing evidence that there might be a cure, but to find it, he's going to have to get out of jail, get out of the country, and track down the man responsible. He can't do any of that alone, but he also can't rely on any of his non-human friends for help, not when they're all getting sick.

What he needs is a particularly gifted human, who can do things no other human is capable of. He knows one such person. He calls himself a fixer, and he's Adam's—and possibly the world's—last hope. That's provided he believes any of it.

Immortal: Last Call is the sixth book in the *Immortal Novel Series*, and also the end of a long journey for one immortal man.

❧

Immortal Stories

❧

Eve

"...if your next question is, what could that possibly make me, if I'm not an angel or a god? The answer is the same as what I said before: many have considered me a god, and probably a few have thought of me as an angel. I'm neither, if those positions are defined by any kind of supernormal magical power. True magic of that kind doesn't exist, but I can do things that may appear magic to someone slightly more tethered to their mortality. I'm a woman, and that's all. What may make me different from the next woman is that it's possible I'm the very first one..."

For most of humankind, the woman calling herself Eve has been nothing more than a shock of red hair glimpsed out of the corner of the eye, in a crowd, or from a great distance. She's been worshipped, feared, and hunted, but perhaps never understood. Now, she's trying to reconnect with the world, and finding that more challenging than anticipated.

Can the oldest human on Earth rediscover her own humanity? Or will she decide the world isn't worth it?

~

The Immortal Chronicles

~

Immortal at Sea (volume 1)

Adam's adventures on the high seas have taken him from the Mediterranean to the Barbary Coast, and if there's one thing he learned, it's that maybe the sea is trying to tell him to stay on dry land.

~

Hard-Boiled Immortal (volume 2)

The year was 1942, there was a war on, and Adam was having a lot of trouble avoiding the attention of some important people. The kind of people with guns, and ways to make a fella disappear. He was caught somewhere between the mob and the government, and the only way out involved a red-haired dame he was pretty sure he couldn't trust.

Immortal and the Madman (volume 3)

On a nice quiet trip to the English countryside to cope with the likelihood that he has gone a little insane, Adam meets a man who definitely has. The madman's name is John Corrigan, and he is convinced he's going to die soon.

He could be right. Because there's trouble coming, and unless Adam can get his own head together in time, they may die together.

Yuletide Immortal (volume 4)

When he's in a funk, Adam the immortal man mostly just wants a place to drink and the occasional drinking buddy. When that buddy turns out to be Santa Claus, Adam is forced to face one of the biggest challenges of extremely long life: Christmas cheer. Will Santa break him out of his bad mood? Or will he be responsible for depressing the most positive man on the planet?

Regency Immortal (volume 5)

Adam has accidentally stumbled upon an important period in history: Vienna in 1814. Mostly, he'd just like to continue to enjoy the local pubs, but that becomes impossible when he meets Anna, an intriguing woman with an unreasonable number of secrets and sharp objects.

Anna is hunting down a man who isn't exactly a man, and if Adam doesn't help her, all of Europe will suffer. If Adam *does* help, the cost may be his own life. It's not a fantastic set of options. Also, he's probably fallen in love with her, which just complicates everything.